THE REFUGEES

A Novel About Heroism, Suffering, Human Values,
Morality and Sacrifices of People During a War

Daniel Churchill (a.k.a. Zvezdan Ćurčić)

authorHOUSE®

AuthorHouse™
1663 Liberty Drive
Bloomington, IN 47403
www.authorhouse.com
Phone: 1 (800) 839-8640

Published by AuthorHouse 08/07/2015

ISBN: 978-1-5049-2762-8 (sc)
ISBN: 978-1-5049-2763-5 (hc)
ISBN: 978-1-5049-2761-1 (e)

Library of Congress Control Number: 2015912613

Print information available on the last page.

Any people depicted in stock imagery provided by Thinkstock are models, and such images are being used for illustrative purposes only. Certain stock imagery © Thinkstock.

This book is printed on acid-free paper.

Based on memories and notes of grandpa
Milich Dragovich (Milić Dragović)

To all who have suffered and are suffering the effects of war

Uncle Krsto

It was late spring in 1917. Seventy-five-year-old Krsto tapped a stick on the chapped, heavy door of Staniya's home. Krsto was a tall, skinny man, slightly curved with broad shoulders and a big, loose, grizzled mustache. A large, aquiline nose and thick eyebrows, which towered over his eyes, revealed the rough look of a highlander from Montenegro's karsts. In fact he was a good-natured old man, despite being crushed by poverty, impoverishment, bitter hardships, and hard farmwork.

When he moved from Montenegro to Toplica, he was about forty years old and still unmarried. Upon arrival at Bechov Karst (Bećov Krš), he found several families from his old countryside. He quickly became a close friend to them. In a small dell below Bechov Karst, he built a wooden hut with only one room. He plastered it with mud and covered it with beech boards he cut, carved, and processed to make it waterproof.

In the middle of the hut, he placed a sizable number of flat stones to make into his new home's fireplace. Between the beams above the fireplace, he positioned a strong pole made from a cer tree, on which he hung large chains (verige) to hold cooking dishes he brought from Montenegro.

Around Uncle Krsto's hut was dense forest on all sides, from which a small island peeped. There had been many stories and legends about this karst. It was told that, on the night of a full moon, fires and evil spirits were jumping around it, dropping various sounds, playing some unknown instruments, and calling some of the settlers' names.

Some talked about how they witnessed a vision of red silk, which fell from the top down and behind tree branches, before sunset. Others claimed they listened to a crying child around midnight. Yet others said they watched kids jumping and moving across the karst in the moonlight and listened to the bleating and scratching of claws on the rocks.

Although he had heard all these stories about Bechov Karst, Uncle Krsto decided to settle right there under the karst to build his wooden hut. No one knew what guided him to become a neighbor of the unholy, but after his hut emerged, no one at Bechov Karst noticed anything unusual any longer.

The new neighbor of Bechov Karst soon married a beautiful, dark-haired woman named Lucia, who soon bore him a son, Masho, and another child, a girl who soon died afterward of smallpox. Masho grew and developed into a burly guy. He was as tall as his father was, and black curly hair and a thin, black mustache adorned his head. Lucia died when he was sixteen years old, and since then they had no female in the house.

Masho married Miruna right after the family gave Lucia the first-year commemoration after her death. Young Miruna bore a son to Masho, Dyoko, who was only five years old when Masho hung a colorful wool bag on his shoulder, embraced a Turkish shooting rifle, and headed to Merdare with uncertainty to join the Serbo-Turkish war. Uncle Krsto stayed with his daughter-in-law Miruna and grandson Dyoko.

Staniya, a small, dark-haired woman from the city of Pech in Metohia, was about twenty-five years old when the Turkish War broke out and Stevan went with the others to Merdare to join the Serbian fighters. She was left with three small children, of whom the eldest was five and the youngest was just a year old.

Staniya looked over the house and nursed the children, and she never complained of loneliness or adversity. She attended to all male affairs: plowing, harvesting the crops, turning the heavy grindstone wheel, milling flower, cutting wood for fires, carrying wood on her backside, and feeding dozens of red goats and a cow. She was eloquent and open as well as free and brave. And above all, she had good character, always cheerful and smiling, and she was a loyal wife and mother. She had a small body, and she was attractive and beautifully built.

Staniya jumped up and opened the door, and she was pleasantly surprised when she saw the old man, Uncle Krsto.

"God help you, young woman," said Krsto with a gentle smile.

"God bless you, Uncle Krsto. Come sit and relax." Staniya moved aside from the door to allow the man to enter.

Uncle Krsto entered, put his stick against the wall, and sat down in a small tripod chair that Staniya passed to him. He pulled a smoking pipe made of clay from his pocket, and he filled it with tobacco. Staniya carefully held a piece of ember to help Uncle Krsto light the tobacco. The man pulled two to three puffs, and blue smoke and the stench of mold and nicotine filled the room. Staniya flung open the door and placed another tripod chair against it so it would not close.

Outside was a summer day. The sun baked the land as if it were August, although it was only the end of June. A large, thin dog was gasping with his tongue hanging out, defending himself from aggressive flies that had been savagely attacking his eyes and mouth. Chickens were almost collapsing from thirst as they revolved around the empty tap made of a piece of oak tree that formerly served to feed pigs. The chickens clumsily excavated remainders of food and liquid.

"How are you, Staniya? How are the kids?" The man crossed his left leg over his right knee.

"Praise God, Uncle, we're alive and there's still something to eat. God forbid it get worse, but we will manage to make it another day. How are you, old man? Did you hear anything from Masho?"

"I do not know anything, Staniya. I was told he survived Albania and typhoid, and now he is somewhere in Thessaloniki with the Allied armies. Something is being prepared there, but only God knows what and how."

"Let's just hope in God's name that he is alive and healthy back there. We are used to suffering around here already. If it weren't for those Bulgarian dogs, we would somehow be all right, but we are in constant fear and uncertainty because of them. And it seems that time is not passing by quickly enough. I heard they ravaged Racha; even women were not left in peace." She raised a coffee pot from the stove, poured a cup of hot liquid made from barley, and gave it to Uncle Krsto. "Take the cup, old man. It's from barley, but we got used to it. It's good when there is no real coffee."

"Oh, thank you, my dear Staniya. I have not had a cup of it for more than ten days. There is no sugar, and nowhere can it be obtained around here, even if we had a lot of money to pay for it. No one can even go buy it in Koorshoomliya. It's too far to go there in this hot, terrible weather."

The dog in the yard violently jerked a rusty chain and grunted.

Staniya ran to the door and then immediately turned and whispered, "A Chetnick!"

"What kind of Chetnick at this time?" muttered Uncle Krsto, as if he were saying it to himself. He stood up and leaned against the doorframe.

A well-built man on a horse approached the gate of Staniya's yard. His small horse was typical for those seen in the mountainous regions in Serbia. The tall and broad-shouldered man might have been about twenty-five years old. The sun and wind had tanned him. He had a thin, black mustache and black curly hair, which he had carelessly pushed under a tilted fur hat, which presented him as more handsome and imposing.

He wore a pinstriped peasant suit, still in good condition, and short leather boots, above which Serbian woolen embroidered socks could be seen. Below the open-necked short coat were crossed bandoliers of ammunition. A short Serbian cavalry carbine was hanging over his left shoulder, and a Montenegrin revolver was positioned under his belt.

He directed the horse through the open gate and walked to the door of the house. "God bless you, good people," he greeted.

"May God give you all the best, young man," Staniya and Uncle Krsto answered as if with one voice.

"Come. Sit down and have a rest," said Uncle Krsto in a hoarse voice. "Tell me what good news you are bringing to us today. I hope you have something good to tell us, my son."

"I have, and I do not," answered the man. "Kosta Pechanac raised us against the Bulgarians, and we very well smashed our heads against the hard wall and are perishing like hunted rabbits. Many of the enemy soldiers perished; however, a lot of us died too."

"And what happened with Kosta?" the old man asked, keen to know. "I hope he continues his fight against the evil dogs."

"He is somewhere wandering around the Radan Mountains, and he hides like a coward. He is planning something, but no one is there to support him. The Bulgarians are searching for him, but the old fox remains artfully hidden. He wants to raise a major revolt with a handful of people against so many foreign forces, and many of our innocent people died."

The Chetnick pulled a small pouch of tobacco from his pocket, tailored a cigarette in a piece of yellow paper, and offered the pouch to the old man. "Take it, Uncle. It's from our homeland, the city of Vranje."

"Thank you, my son." The old man extended his hand toward the tobacco pouch. "Where are you from, my son?"

"Yablanica (Jablanica), Uncle. I am the son of a forester Milosh (Miloš), if you've heard of him. He was a forester, and he often crisscrossed this region. You should know him. My name is Sreten."

"Milosh foresters?" muttered the old man. "I used to know Milosh very well. He was a good man, like no other. But I heard that lightning killed him?"

"That's right, Uncle. He was harvesting in the field, and a storm came along. He hid under an old oak, and lighting snapped in the midst of it. The man was destroyed in a flash, as if he never existed."

"God rest his soul." Tears filled the old man's eyes.

"Come on. I will get a little something ready for lunch. You must be hungry?" asked Staniya, who was until that moment silently observing the strange man and listening to the conversation.

"Thank you, ma'am, but I have to hurry. I have some urgent business in Vaseeljevic (Vasiljevac) to attend to, and I'm going to eat something there. But we got into this talk, and the time does not wait. I have to move on. Good-bye and God bless you."

"Good-bye, my son, and may God take care of you," Uncle Krsto said in a sad voice.

"Good-bye and have a pleasant time," Staniya added.

The man nudged the horse with his boots and soon sank into the woods via a narrow, winding path. Uncle Krsto took his stuff and said good-bye to Staniya. Taking difficult, uncertain steps, he walked in the direction of Bechov Karst.

War and Toplica's Uprising

Sometime in the second half of the nineteenth century, Serbs from Serbia and Montenegro settled regions east of the then-Turkish border and the region of Kosovo and Metohia. Then emerged border villages, including Pravitica, Matarova, Merdare, Vaseechevac (Vasićevac), Cat's Rock (Mačja Stena), Trpeze, Prekorodye (Prekorođe), Dobry Do (Dobri Do), and others. Colonization was followed by an agreement of the Serbian and Montenegrin governments in order to block penetration of the Turks from Kosovo on Serbian territory, which had recently been liberated after nearly five hundred years of Ottoman occupation.

Residing in the mountainous areas covered with high, dense, and old forests of oaks, beech, and other trees, these settlers, facing poverty, were exposed to various hardships, sufferings, misery, and difficulties. It was necessary to cut and clear the century-old mountain forest, creating scarce fields for planting crops, primitive huts, or house chalets, usually covered with rye straw, wooden tiles, or leaves of fern. The little livestock of animals they had, often brought from the old homelands in Montenegro and Western Serbia, was exposed to frequent slaughter by many wild beasts from these huge forests around them.

People were keeping almost as many dogs as sheep in fenced houses with high fences and sharpened poles. And on the back side lay various traps and pits to capture beasts, but the results were more or less negligible.

Over time people beat nature's forces. Fields and meadows were growing; forests were being narrowed. Here and there sprouted cabins and huts plastered with mud, mixed with wheat chaff, and then painted with white lime (processed limestone). Rarely some houses with red roof tiles could be seen. The square windows were so small that a human head could barely squeeze through. They were glazed with everything, just not real glass. In many places there was no window glass. Sometimes stretched kid or lamb skin, which had previously been scraped or shaved, closed these windows.

These huts were often torched and burned to the ground, causing such fiery flames that could not be quenched. Houses were built on isolated estates, making them quite distant from one another, preventing people from quickly helping each other in cases of emergency.

The life of these settlers was difficult and painful, especially in the initial stages of settlement. They were clearing the forest, plowing with wooden plows or digging witch picks and hoes, and operating grinding mills by hand-turning a heavy rock, in which were scarce grains of corn, barley, wheat, or helda beans. They fought with beasts and interruptions from the other side of the old border.

Crags and vast distance from urban areas and other aspects were further hampering lives of these highlanders. But there were pleasant moments once they had been forgotten life problems. Especially in the winter evenings, the people met at gatherings where they were playing, joking, singing with fiddles, and often remaining so until just before dawn. And during the feast days they met, they were competing in throwing stones from their shoulders, jumping in the long jumps, sport shooting with guns, and performing other knightly games. Shooting here was the most popular sport in which they had experience since childhood.

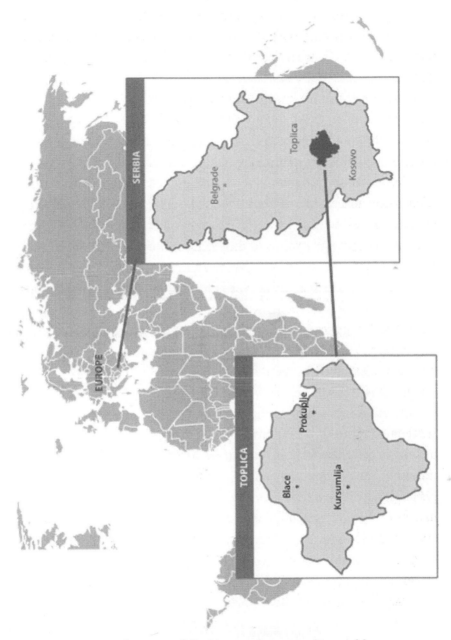

*The Toplica district and Serbia are shown on this world map.
Toplica is positioned in the southern part of Serbia. It has a
population of 91,754 and was named after the Toplica River.*

A difficult life, conquest of the nature, and a spectrum of other problems tempered and strengthened these people from early childhood. Difficult mountain winters, huge snow and fog, and swollen streams and rivers did not break their spirit, morale, pride, and desire to remain and forever settle on the lean mountainous country land, often timidly carried by rains, swollen creeks, and rivers.

The Serbian population from the Kosovo and Metohia (occupied by Turkey in those days prior to the Balkan Wars) often shifted across the border to the Serbian side to cry and complain of the Turkish oppression and check if they would soon receive any material or military help. Toplica's people always fraternally welcomed these people, feasted, and promised they had not forgotten them. But times had passed, and everything remained the same. Turks and Arnauts (Albanians) were penetrating Serbian territory, and Serbs were on the Turkish side as well. Both were looting cattle, killing, and robbing each other, and so from day to day, that created and deepened the growing hostility.

As 1912 arrived, along the border, especially in Merdare, rumbled the famous Serbo-Turkish War, or First Balkan War. At night the flames of cannons and grenades tore the sky. Women loaded with stuff were rushing to the border, carrying food, clothes, and other necessities to their fathers, husbands, and sons. The dogs were sadly howling; the ravens were croaking and hurrying on fresh human corpses. Children and the elderly stayed on the high ridges at night, hearing terrible roars of the war and watching flame of grenades and burning buildings at the border and further away from it.

The Turkish Empire, torn apart by red tape bureaucracy and long wars, had not been able to seriously resist the resentful Serbian warriors. The Turkish army retreated, giving less resistance here and there, and it was soon expelled from Kosovo and Metohia. The war soon spread into Macedonia and Southeastern Serbia, resulting in the Serbo-Bulgarian War, or Second Balkan War. And right after that, the Great War (or First World War, as it is known today) began.

Overpowered by Austro-Hungarian and Bulgarian armies, the Serbian troops retreated via Albania down to the Greek island of Corfu. And they later established the front line with the aid of allies from the Adriatic Sea in Albania to the northeastern parts of Greece in Macedonia near the Greek city of Tessaloniki. That front line became known as the famous Salonika Front.

In the border villages in Toplica remained women, old men, and children. Thin, steep, small farm fields remained uncultivated and deserted. Supplies of livestock were approaching the end, and soon total hunger appeared in this area. Frequent incursions of Arnaut gangs from Kosovo, Bulgarian irregulars known as Komite, and regular Bulgarian army, which occupied Toplica, slayed those few cattle and sheep left.

Serbian army deserters represented another kind of danger. These self-proclaimed guerilla fighters did not have anything in common with Serbian Chetnicks. The Chetnicks were genuinely resisting the occupiers, while the deserters were bandits who were cleverly finding, stealing, and hiding buried valuables and weapons, looting from abandoned houses, slaughtering (usually sheep and pigs), and performing various other crimes. People feared and hid from those bandits.

Skinny dogs, released from their chains, were rushing around the cabins, frantically barking and growling. Wolves, foxes, and other beasts increased in numbers. Wolves often hosted concerts at night in the surrounding forest ridges, which caused even more growling and howling of frightened dogs. Women and elderly were often alone at night with ardent embers dispersing hungry beasts, who were not reluctant to tear a dog in pieces at the very doorstep of a house or pull remaining sheep out of a stable.

Toward the end of 1916 came Kosta Pechanac, a Serbian army officer from the Salonika Front, and he descended by plane to the plateau of the Radan Mountain, intending to organize the people in Toplica and Yablanica regions to rise and, in this way, weaken the Bulgarian resistance at the Salonika Front.

Kosta Pechanac with a group of Chetnicks

The people of Toplica, fed up with the Bulgarian occupation and atrocities, were barely waiting for the uprising and determined to take revenge. Thus it began in masses to respond to Kosta's call. Most of the insurgents consisted of older people and, even for such a venture, immature young men or women, while far fewer were true warriors. The real warriors who survived the Turkish and Bulgarian wars, bloody battles at Tser (Cer), Guchevo (Gučevo) and other fronts, ordeals of the epic retreat march via Albania, typhoid, and many other hardships were somewhere at the Salonika Front, waiting their time for revenge and liberation of the homeland. Treacherous attacks and shoved knives in the back of Serbia by their Slavic fellow Bulgarians were not allowed to remain unpunished.

In early February 1917, an uprising broke out in Toplica, the only revolt in any of the territories in Europe occupied by the Central Powers forces. Avengers, although poorly armed and equipped, were fiercely storming the far superior Bulgarian army, and soon the enemy was forced to withdraw. In a very short time, the entire region of Kosanica around the Kosanica River in Toplica, the upper part of the Yablanica and Toplica, and the towns of Koorshoomliya and Prokuplje were liberated. The next was the city of Leskovac, where strong enemy forces were concentrated.

However strong Bulgarian and Austro-Hungarian troops and Bulgarian and Albanian irregulars attacked the rebellious forces, who were numerically and technically weakened. Finally they were defeated, which suppressed the uprising in Toplica, and subsequent reprisals resulted in the murder of tens of thousands of Toplica's inhabitants. But even after the defeat, the enemy was not left alone. Individuals and smaller groups of Chetnicks were often harassing the Bulgarian occupiers and inflicted tangible losses upon them.

Death of the Beautiful Pava

The whole area in Kosanica knew how pretty and wonderful Pava, Radoye's (Radoje) wife, was. Almost everyone admired her for her beauty. When she appeared as a young girl in the village festivals at Becho's Church (Bećova Crkva) in Degrmen village, young and old, both male and female, turned their heads after her. Heavy black braids, always carefully strung together, reached the bottom of her slender waist and provoked sighs of many guys who did not have the courage to approach her. She had thin black eyebrows gracefully matched with her slanted black eyes. Her face was flushed like an apple face, and her teeth were snow white. She had graceful posture, a warm and feminine voice, and beautiful and restrained behavior. All made this young and lovely girl more beautiful.

She was the only child in her family, yet she was not spoiled. She was working all the housework, except farm work, which she had not been asked to attend to. Her father and Uncle Stanko cultivated the little land they had, and Stanko's children usually looked after the cattle. She had the first proposal for marriage when she was just fifteen years old, but her parents had not given her because they found it difficult to separate from her. She married Radoye on the eve of the Serbo-Turkish war when she was barely seventeen years old.

Radoye, a well-built country boy, was older than Pava by about eight years. He was strong with firm facial features and stood at a medium height. He had little to say, but his every spoken utterance was decidedly appropriate and in place. No one in the area could bring him down in wrestling or throw a stone from shoulders further than he could. He knew how to sing well along with the traditional, single-string Serbian instrument called goosle (gusle). Young and old people were happy to be in company with him and invite him over for gatherings.

Despite the enormous power he possessed, he never even once ended up in a fight or argument with anyone. Pava's parents loved and respected him, and they were glad when he appeared as her fiancé and gladly gave them their blessings to marry.

When the Serbo-Turkish war came along, Radoye was among the first to go to the war. He served in the army before the war and was promoted to the rank of a reserve sergeant. Between the Serbo-Turkish and Bulgarian wars, he came home for a few days and then immediately returned to his command in the city of Nish (Niš).

Throughout the Serbian-Bulgarian and First World War, no one knew anything about him. From only one letter from his friend in Trpeze that arrived sometime in 1916, Pava learned he was alive and promoted to the upper rank. After that she knew nothing about him; nor would she ever know anything, although she constantly dreamed about him, especially because they had no children.

It was a dry and warm September day in 1917. The air smelled of rotten fruit and seared corn. All over the upper Kosanica, fear and uncertainty hung. The Bulgarians increased their patrols, and soldiers roamed the villages around the clock. And in every house they encountered, they sought to eat. Just in one day, said the villagers, they ate lunch at five houses in the village. People called them scavengers and stayed away from them wherever possible.

They really looked like scavengers. Often short, dark, and overweight, they were a nuisance to the village wherever they went. Young women and girls took shelter in front of them, and often charcoal-blackened and mud-stained faces and dirty clothes tried to show them as uglier than what they actually were.

On that fateful day, Pava's mother-in-law Tominka called Pava, who was slightly tidying up the house, and said to her, "Pava, dear daughter, get ready and go to Yelica (Jelica), Petar's wife, and ask her to give you the tool to process that little wool we have left over. If it stays there under the roof, mice will be making nests in it. They will completely destroy it, and it will all go to waste."

"Okay, Mother, I will do it. Just let me finish this cooking I am doing right now."

Petar's house was located about a half hour walk away, and it was necessary to cross a deep creek, which lay between two valleys overgrown with tall beech forests. Adults and children avoided this place at night, and hardly anyone would even go to this place alone, even during the day. An old watermill was there. Who knew when and who built it.

It was told that an old man named Vidak, when he passed near the watermill at night, heard a kid in a bag in a bush besides the road. Vidak thought that some shepherds, who were there during the day guarding goats, forgot it. And the old man started to look for the kid. Once he had found it, he grabbed its front and back legs and placed it at the back of his neck in order to take it home and to inquire whose it might be the next day.

But Vidak did not come home that night. When roosters first announced the daylight, Vidak was found riding on a curved willow, which overlooked the deep green vortex of the creek. Of course there was no sign of the kid. The old man fell sick and soon died, taking the mystery behind the kid and willow over the green vortex to his grave.

There were other stories about this old watermill. Someone named Yoko Punishin (Joko Punišin) lost a cow and then went to look for it. Sometime in the late evening, he arrived at the watermill and heard music and drums. He paused, wondering why there was a wedding party at this time of the night. Soon the wedding party surrounded Yoko and started a traditional Serbian folk dance, holding hands and forming a circle around him. At the top of the round was a young bride. Yoko was led by the young bride and offered rakiya (a Serbian beverage with high alcoholic content usually distilled from plum or pear fruits).

A whole baked pie dish was put in front of him. The pie was still hot and very tasty so it simply melted in Yoko's mouth. When dawn finally arrived, there was no sign of a wedding party and the young bride. Only one sizeable piece of cow dung, partly eaten, was lying in front of Yoko.

Pava was walking via a narrow path that led to the end of the old mill. It was sometime before noon, and there was nothing to fear. Over the left hand, she wore a light yellow basket in which the black ball of wool restlessly raced, sometimes to one and occasionally to the other corner of the bag. She was knitting socks for Radoye.

"Well, let's have a stock of many socks for him …"

When her Radoye returned drowned her thoughts. She thought about Radoye and their first meeting at the festival in Degrmen. She remembered that first heart-shaped cake with a small, rectangular mirror in the middle and a picture of a boy and a girl on the other side that she got as a present from him. Oh, she was so fond of the little cake from Radoye's hands. She would hug it for a long time and secretly examine and kiss it when left alone at home.

She hated and cursed the bloody war, which broke her away from her greatest love, her Radoye. Some dark foreboding was telling her that it would never happen, as it was in the past to hug him and whisper through the night for a long time.

Sharp and brief screams awakened her from her daydreaming.

"Stop!"

She stopped and looked in the direction from where the voice arrived. She saw two Bulgarian soldiers, dirty and underweight. They stood near the old wild pear tree, whose fruit were emerging through the dried yellow leaves.

"Come here!" yelled a younger Bulgarian soldier, giving her the right hand index finger sign to come there.

Pava was lost and stood silently. She unconsciously looked at the Bulgarians. Her heart was pounding so hard that it seemed it would jump out of her chest at any moment. It was like she was paralyzed. She could not move forward or backward.

"Come here now!" she heard an animal-like scream call from the Bulgarian soldiers.

This new call completely awakened her. She quickly made a U-turn to return home but soon felt a strong grip on her right arm. A

Bulgarian roughly jerked and pulled her toward his friend, who was still standing, leaning his back against the wild pear.

"Lie down!" ordered the Bulgarian, dropping a rifle on the ground, while the other clutched Pava's arm.

Her arm ached. It seemed her blood no longer circulated through her body. Her brain was instantly working. She was thinking of what to do, how to get out of the hands of these rabid dogs, and how to prevent the embarrassment that would be a lifelong following. She was Pava, a proud Serb girl, the one whom many great guys, including her neighbors and her brothers by blood, wished for. She was the loved wife of Radoye, one whom she loved so much and always daydreamed about. She was waiting for his return. But she succumbed to these dammed Bulgarians, hateful enemies, who, like locusts, plundered her country, burned homes, and killed innocent people.

No, never! Alive not ever! Even if it were the last day of her young life. She instantly snatched the hand of the executioner, and with her hands tightly hugged the roughened wild pear tree, she firmly resolved not to let go of it alive all the way long until her hideous enemies were still nearby.

The heavy Bulgarian rifle butts mercilessly fell on her back, head, and arms. She felt warm blood trickling down the fingers of the hands and back of the head, but strong arms grabbed on the pear that she did not even release for a moment. The soldiers lined rough Bulgarian curses, dragged her by the arms and legs, hit her numerous times with rifle butts, and kicked her with their legs. She felt her ribs breaking. She knew how her power faded. She knew she was near her end, but the pride was stronger than the pain and suffering. She had to win or die. The third option was not possible.

Pava suddenly felt how a hard and sharp object penetrated through her chest. She saw the bloodied bayonet tip sticking out of her white blouse from her chest. At the same time, she felt the strong, painful jolt that broke her away from the pear and soon found herself embraced by death, on the ground of her beloved native land, desecrated by the legs of the hated enemy.

She felt she was sinking into the deep, dark bottomless abyss. She whispered Radoye's name, which, as it seemed to be the end of it, he gently stroked her hair and face. Finally all was gone: the abyss, the darkness, and Radoye. Forever had swallowed beautiful Pava, a young and proud, swarthy beauty.

Her body was buried with great regret. Many tales and folk songs lamented this glorious woman. Many tears fell over her dead body. Many long stories were told about her heroic posture and martyrdom.

Bulgarians and Now Arnauts

Bulgarians had their forces mainly settled in the villages of upper Toplica, lower Kosanica, and Yablanica. Occasionally these moved to the highlands, in the direction of the old Turkish border, to calm down the disobedient and rebellious highlanders. Gallows in Topolica were erected in almost every village and regularly very busy. Innocent people were often hanging on them, dangling for a whole week, to the point where the stench was not possible to approach. Swarms of flies buzzed around the gallows, spreading the stench and various sicknesses all over the place. Shepherds were by far avoiding the gallows, holding fingers on their noses and whipping skinny cattle as soon as possible to get out of the stench and swarms of flies.

Bulgarian soldiers executing Serbian villagers

The ground was burned from stench, arson, and typhoid. Bursts of gunfire were paralyzing air and casting fear into the hearts of hungry and feeble people. Day by day, there was an increasing number of sick people with typhus and Spanish fever. Often there was no one to dig the graves or transfer mortals to their eternal home. Medical intervention was not a possibility at all. In fact doctors were in these villages, yet no one had ever seen one, and many had never heard of one. If someone needed to remove a tooth, a farmer pulled it out, using a pair of old, rusty pliers. If someone broke an arm or a leg or if snakes or a rabid dog bit someone, there was always a someone in villages who knew how to treat that. However against Spanish flu or typhoid, there was no help or medicine available at all.

The month of October 1917 was slightly warmer than usual. A few older men and women were coming back from the Kravarsko cemetery, where they buried an old widow named Mariya (Marija), who herself died from Spanish flue. Her only child Milosava, married fifteen years ago in the village of Trn, wailed and wailed, mentioning her father Yovan (Jovan) and brother Milosh (Miloš), who died in a brawl at Merdare before the Turkish War.

Suddenly the people at the funeral heard shots from rifles, first one and then some more. Then they saw smoke at a distance. No smoke itself in this area was an unusual occurrence. But where did the shots come from?

From Cat's Rock, a bareheaded boy with tousled hair rushed over on a bareback horse. When he reached the people at the funeral, he slowed the horse's and slipped off it.

"God bless you people!" said the hoarse boy.

"May God bless you too," all answered. "Where are you going, God willing?"

"Get out, folks! There are Arnauts. They are burning Trpeze, and they will be here soon to kill you all," the confused boy explained. "My grandpa Vuyo (Vujo) sent me to inform you. I'll go to the Bukumir family to tell them about this too. I'm going, people! Stay good with God!"

The villagers looked at each other in surprise and with fear in their eyes. The situation was more than desperate with disease, hunger, pressure, terror of the Bulgarian army, and now Arnauts from Kosovo and Metohia.

"What are we going to do about this, Mother?" Milusha (Miluša), a wife of Vasiliye (Vasilije), asked in a tearful voice.

"What else but to bury and hide our things and take with us what we can with these little animals to run down to Toplica, as long as we can get there?" proposed Uncle Todor, Milusha's seventy-year-old father-in-law.

"There is nothing else left for us to do," all agreed. "We have to move on quickly. In an hour or two, Arnauts might be here. After that it all will be late."

People dispersed, each running to his or her own house. Shepherds chased livestock, and refugees gathered at houses of the Bukumir family. And they hurriedly moved further toward the village of Kutlovo. Women were pulling toddlers by hands and carrying sizeable burdens of things on their backs. More mature children were chasing the distressed animals, which were hard to settle down. Cattle were stabbing each other, roaring and kicking. Old people carried some of their things, mainly that which they held most dear.

So Uncle Todor carried the portrait of King Peter I wrapped in an old, yellowed newspaper through which a white moustache protruded, and it seems as if the whole painting were made of that moustache alone.

The refugees were slowly moving. Little kids were screaming, while burdens hampered the movement. Livestock were tired and a little bit calmed down. And for the children, they were easier to control. When they arrived at Devil's Creek (Đavolji potok), they decided to camp and spend the night there and perhaps stay a little longer to rest. They tied cattle, horses, and donkeys to the beech trees, removed the loads, and settled to rest in peace comfortably.

Hunger was strong, but nobody dared to first pull out something from their bags.

Finally Uncle Todor said, "Come on, Vasiliye, my son. Catch that sheep and slaughter it. Let us eat it before the Bulgarians take it from us."

Vasiliye, a scrawny man in his forties, was the son of Uncle Todor. When he was seven years old, he fell from a cherry tree and broke his right leg above the knee and received spinal injuries. For a long time, he was lying in a hospital in Nish, where his plastered leg somehow healed but the backbone remained flawed. The drafting committee in the Serbian army deemed him permanently unfit for service.

When he turned twenty-five years old, he married a poor, but quite hardworking and honest, Milusha (Miluša), daughter of the widow Staniya Vasilyevich (Stanija Vasiljević). She bore him two children. Quiet by nature, Vasiliye was loved and respected, regardless of his physical flaw. And in his village of Prekorodye (Prkorođe), he was elected to be the village head. Although he was self-taught, he knew how to read well, so women and the elderly often visited him with arrival of letters from the front line. He hated the Bulgarians above all, complaining that he was not healthy to fight with them, even if that culminated in his death.

Vasiliye got up, took a sizable knife, dragged its blade over firesteel (ognjilo) several times to sharpen it, and yelled, "Jump, my dear! Grab that sheep and hold it down so I can slaughter it!"

"No, Daddy, please!" his ten-year old daughter, almost in tears, begged. She loved Kalusha (Kaluša) more than all the other sheep.

"Come on. Come on. Do not cry like a little baby, but grab that sheep as I told you," Vasiliye said, pretending to be angry.

"I'm going to do it, Uncle Vasiliye. Just tell me which one to catch!" asserted thirteen-year-old Yovan, grandson of Uncle Marko.

Yovan was growing up quite nicely for his age and developed well. As a little boy, he dragged much of the household work on his puny shoulders. When he was eleven years old, he began to plow, cut trees, and perform other manual work of adults.

When Vasiliye showed him the sheep to catch, he skillfully sneaked up, grabbed it, and knocked it over. Vasiliye dragged a knife across its throat, and when the sheep calmed down, he began to scream. All children from the refugee camp gathered together and curiously watched the sheep at one moment and another at Vasiliye and his bloodied hands. They felt sorry for the sheep but were anxious to have a taste of a good, warm meal.

Avenger Sreten

Sreten, our well-known Chetnick, sat in Trpeze's forest and was studying the yellow, oil-contaminated, folding map of Serbia. His swift mountain horse was eating oats from a small bag perched on its head (zobnica). A short Serbian cavalry carbine was leaning against the oak, within reach of his hands. His large handgun was sticking out from his waist belt. Bandoliers of ammunition were lying beside him, not to bother his resting and map reading.

It was noon when the crying of women and screaming of children from Cat's Rock reached his ears. He thought someone had fallen victim to typhus, as was often the case in this area. So he continued to look at the map and some notes from a small pocket notebook framed in a rough piece of tanned leather. But something was not right.

Cries and screams from the direction of Cat's Rock went on and on. Sreten even heard an adult man cry, scream, and threaten as well, from which he recognized that this was not an ordinary typhus death. He folded the map and small pocket notebook, stuffed them into the inside pocket of his coat, girded his bandoliers, put the rifle over his head and across his upper body, and removed a small bag full of grass attached to the horse's mouth that it was feeding on. He saddled and mounted the animal.

When he arrived at Cat's Rock, he found many people gathered over the mutilated body of a swarthy young woman. Clotted blood was in her black hair and on her snow-white blouse and chest. The fingers of the hands were tortured and broken.

"What is this, people?" Sreten cried at the crowd, who did not even notice his presence.

The crowd noise died down a bit. All eyes pointed at the stranger, his horse, and weapons.

Finally Uncle Krsto spoke, "The evil, my son, that is not remembered around here. What else! They, the Bulgarian dogs, killed our innocent child. May God judge them without mercy. They failed to carry out their ill intention to rape this child, and this is the way they laid vengeance on her."

Uncle Krsto dragged Sretena aside and told him about all the particulars he learned about the crime. He said, early that morning, some had seen two Bulgarian soldiers coming down from Cow's Head (Kravarske Glavice), toward Cat's Rock's stream, in the direction of an old mill, where this ruthless crime was committed.

"Has anyone seen them here in the village?" asked Sreten.

"No, no! They did not enter the village, but it seems they went back after the crime. Soon a boy from the village arrived here. I think it was Nedya (Neđa), and he told us he saw two Bulgarian soldiers just above the village of Little Vucha (Mala Vuča). I believe those are the two villains."

The old man began to look across the crowd of people, and once he saw the boy, he cried, "Petrashin (Petrašin)! Come here! We are going to ask you something."

A boy of about twelve years of age, pale and white-livered, approached them. "What do you want to ask me, Grandfather?"

Sreten dismounted from his horse and tied it to a stake at the fence. Then he began questioning the boy, "Where have you been today?"

"I was at my aunt's place in Ivan Tower (Ivan Kula). That's where I spent the night, and this morning I left for home via Little Vucha."

"And have you met anyone on your way?" asked Sreten.

"I met three elderly women on the road near the village of Zebice, and once I passed Little Vucha, I saw two Bulgarian soldiers. I hid in the woods and watched until they were disappearing along the creek and heading deep into the forest. As they passed I saw one was covered with blood. They were talking, laughing, and pushing each other jokingly, but I did not understand what they were saying. I met no one else on the way."

Sreten released the boy and thoughtfully stared at the old man, Uncle Krsto, and the crowd. And at the end, his gaze wandered somewhere down Cat's Rock's stream and toward the blue heights of mountains around Ivan Tower. For a moment he was remembering his past and childhood. He remembered when he was at the foot of the Radan Mountain with a group of boys and girls minding sheep and picking wild strawberries and red bouquets of flower, which he carried home to please his mother.

He recalled the early bachelorhood and village festivals, which the people freely attended. He thought of flute and popular round dances, in which necklaces jangled on young and lovely girls. He remembered that dear and loved freedom swallowed by the savage forces of the hated enemies—the German, Austro-Hungarian, and Bulgarians occupiers.

"Ah, Bulgarians, Bulgarians!" thought Sreten. "You are the largest evil that happened to us in our history, but we will mercilessly avenge for all your crimes and wrongdoings, even at the cost of our own lives."

A woman whispered something in Uncle Krsto's ear, and then he invited in Sreten for discussion in a small wooden cottage. There they found a table with food ready to be eaten, including a frying pan full of yellow, but still warm, gruel.

They all sat down and had a little bit to eat. Somehow there was a bottle with some not-so-fresh rakiya made of pears.

The old man lifted the bottle, crossed himself, and toasted, "For the eternal rest of Pava's soul, let God bless her with the kingdom of heaven, and let our enemies get the punishment they deserve from God's hands." He drank two sips from the bottle and then passed it to Sreten.

Sreten accepted the bottle, drank a bit, took a few bites of food, and then stood up. "Uncle, I have to go. Difficult tasks are awaiting me." He grabbed Uncle Krsto's hand and shook it.

The old man said, "May God follow you wherever you go, my son. May we meet again in a better mood and occasion than today."

Sreten greeted the attendees, climbed on the horse, and soon rode off and sank deep into the forest along Cat's Rock's creek. A bunch of people gathered for a long time, watching this burly guy and thinking about him and his fate.

As they vented their anger against the unfortunate and innocent Pava, the Bulgarian soldiers walked down the creek in the direction of Little Vucha. Once they spotted a village, they paused to look at the houses and then picked one that would best accommodate their further ill-minded plans. They decided to approach a house, from which a woman came out and was fearfully staring at them.

One soldier spotted a few chickens, and once they saw a big, red rooster, he grabbed his rifle and took aim. The rifle fired, and the rooster jumped up and fell to the ground with outstretched wings. A woman stopped her breath in fear. Motionless as paralyzed, she stood voiceless and dull, looking into the rooster that was lying motionlessly.

Pointing at the rooster, one of the soldiers shouted, "Cook it, you stupid women!" His eyes shone with pleasure and anger at the same time.

The woman was even more confused and scared and then pulled herself together. She picked up the dead rooster and brought it into the house.

She silently whispered, "May your eyes cook in flames, you damn Bulgarian dogs."

The soldiers entered the house, and one threw himself on a roughly hewn bed made of beech wood and a mattress filled with dry corn leaves. A boy of about seven years old and a somewhat younger girl fearlessly ran out of the house and disappeared somewhere in the neighboring yards.

"Rakiya! Give us rakiya now!" imperiously yelled one of the soldiers at the woman, who was trying to clean the rooster in hot water.

"We do not have any rakiya, sir. Your army drank all of it," answered the frightened woman.

"Find it, or your house will burn in flames! We will kill you all!"

The woman dropped the rooster and quickly headed out to neighboring houses to look for rakiya.

A gloomy autumn dusk swallowed the forested peaks of high mountains and, like a thief, quietly descended over Little Vucha. Somewhere below the village, a loud noise of the rammed Kosanica River could be heard. From some beech tree not far from the village arrived the balanced sound of an owl.

Sreten dismounted from his horse, tied it to thick undergrowth, and calmly smoked a large cigarette wrapped in a newspaper. Mosquitoes were attacking him vigorously, of which he was defending himself with a leafy beech twig.

In the house across a small creek, distant about fifty meters, he heard the murmur of human voices. Somewhere on the other side of the village, he heard barking and then the immediate sad howls of a dog. A small window of the house, from where the voices were drifting, betrayed the weak light of a keroscnc lamp.

Suddenly the noise from the hut across the creek increased. Then Sreten's ear heard the sound of a female scream. And he understood the words, "Let me go. Let me go, damn dogs!"

Male voices could not be understood. He jumped up, grabbed the rifle, ran across the stream, and found himself at the small square window of the hut. He could not see through the stained glass clearly, so he decided to do inside. He pulled open the outer door and immediately pushed open the inner door of the room. A cocked rifle was held ready for action. The scene before him surprised Sreten.

A Bulgarian soldier was holding the woman around the neck, trying to bring her down on her back. The other was pulling her legs toward a bed. The woman fought hard and struggled. She was red to her ears. Her scarf slipped from her head and tightened around her neck. Her tangled brown hair was mcssy. She was about thirty-five to forty years old.

Taken with the woman, the soldiers did not notice Sreten. Their rifles were leaning against the wall, and military belts were also placed somewhere around the room.

Sreten pointed the rifle at them and cried in a very loud voice, "Hands in the air!"

The soldiers froze instantly.

"I said hands up!" again rumbled Sreten.

Both soldiers unquestioningly raised their hands in the air.

"Turn to the wall and hold your hands up! No matter what else you try, you will be killed," thundered Sreten in a commanding voice.

They turned and stood against the wall, not dropping their hands.

"Woman! Ropes quickly!" firmly commanded Sreten to the woman.

The woman ran past him and soon returned with two beef halters.

"Tie them firmly!"

The woman pulled the hands of the first soldier close together and tied them behind his back. She pushed him onto the bed and then tied the second one.

"Put their weapons over there, outside of the house!" Sreten instructed her, not lowering the rifle pointed at the Bulgarian soldiers.

The woman collected the two rifles, took them out of the house, and then returned for the belts.

"Sit down!" Sreten ordered the soldiers.

When they sat down on the ground floor, he swung his rifle over his left shoulder and began removing the soldiers' bayonets. Immediately he observed dried blood on one of the bayonets. Clearly the same bayonet had penetrated the body of the young and innocent Pava, the most beautiful woman of this area, just a few hours ago.

He stopped for a moment and mentally reconstructed the entire event of the violence against Pava. He imagined it in the way that the villagers from Cat's Rock described. He seemed to be looking at the top of that bayonet as Pava's blood soaked from the chest of that glorious and unfortunate women who sacrificed what was most important, her life, to protect her honor and the integrity of her people.

"Quickly find a lantern!" Sreten ordered the woman who could not take her eyes off him and blindly executed all his orders.

"Here's a lantern. I will turn it on," said the woman and began to remove the cylinder. Once the lantern shone, Sreten ordered the soldiers, "Get outside!"

They tremblingly stood up without a word and went where Sreten was pointing. The woman followed Sreten with a lantern in her hand.

Once they came to the water, Sreten ordered them to walk up the creek, which they did for about ten minutes. The narrow village walking path was left far behind. Over his left hand, Sreten was wearing one Bulgarian soldier's belt with a bloodied bayonet. The other belt and rifle remained at the hut.

When they came to a narrow, deep, and complex part of the creek covered with beech bushes, Sreten suddenly pulled out a bloodied bayonet and, with full power, jabbed it in the back of the soldier next to him. Then he snatched the bayonet and instantly jabbed it in the chest of the second soldier, who, frozen, was watching what has happening.

He did not take into account how many times he swung and jabbed the bayonet in their bodies. Revenge for Pava and all the crimes that these bloodsuckers committed to the villages in Kosanica intoxicated him. When he turned he saw the woman with the lantern in her hand, standing still and watching what was happening.

"Are you scared?" asked Sreten.

"Not at all! I would have done the same if I could!"

For a long time, Sreten and the woman dug a grave to hide the bodies of the Bulgarian soldiers. At the end they cut a bundle of three branches and placed these over the fresh grave in order to hide it. If found, that would cause even greater anger and retaliation of the Bulgarian occupiers to unprotected people in Kosanica.

No matter how hard Sreten tried to keep this revenge to the war criminals secret, after two days, it was known to villagers from Cat's Rock, Prekorodye, and Trpeze. Sreten had grown into a hero and legend and was discussed at funerals, festival gatherings, and everywhere the people were getting together. This revenge consecrated beautiful Pava, and the pain in the hearts of her closest was significantly reduced.

Damn Devil's Creek

Devil's Creek was a narrow valley between high mountains, covered with an old beech tree forest. On the east side of the camp were a few lonely country houses, mostly abandoned. Their inhabitants retreated to safer, congregated places with their relatives, friends, and acquaintances. Overgrown tall weeds almost hid the houses. At the door and windows were thick curtains of cobwebs, a testimonial that these were abandoned some time ago.

Only from a single chimney could a weak, bluish column of smoke be seen rising. If the refugees noticed the smoke and residents of the house, certainly they would not camp at this place and would avoid it on their path to safety.

The first morning for the refugees arrived with not-so-good weather. Moisture and fear saturated the air. Dense fog obscured the sun, which was illuminating the wet ground in the valley. Sensing the recent change in the weather, the refugees wanted to extend and speed up their long and uncertain journey as soon as possible. Sheep were dispersed, seeking juicy grass on clear patches of forestland while cattle were still lying tied to the beech trees. Women were huddling around, just starting the fireplace to prepare whatever was available for the breakfast. Uncle Todor, undressed to the waist, was refreshing himself with cold water at a small, clear stream near the camp.

Staniya jokingly interjected, "What is it, old man? Are you planning to get married? This morning you are strengthening your body with cold water."

"No, my daughter. This is what I used to do in the morning every day since childhood, so here and now I am doing it in old age. I like to freshen up, and the mountain stream came to me as ordered."

"That is great, old man! Well, I like to joke so this terrible time before us goes away faster."

In a large cauldron nestled on three sizeable stones simmered thick mutton stew. They believed they would lose all their sheep to the Bulgarian soldiers anyway, so they decided not to starve until they still had a few sheep left around. They did not worry whose sheep were to be slaughtered. They shared all they had. They ate together by sitting on the ground, as field workers or mowers regularly did in the meadows.

Staniya and another girl worked around the fire. Vasiliye brought in dry beech branches and placed them under the cauldron. Bread had been in short supply. They had a little bit of corn flower and should have something to eat until they got down to the Toplica River. And after that, all would be in God's hands.

When they sat down to eat breakfast, a middle-aged woman with two children, a boy of ten and a girl of about eight years old, appeared from somewhere.

"God help you!" greeted the newcomers.

"May God give you all the best," a few voices were heard. "C'mon. Have some breakfast with us since you're there."

"Thank you, but we are not hungry," the woman said, although she and her children were actually quite hungry.

"We did not ask if you were hungry or not," said Uncle Krsto excitingly, "but sit down to eat with us!"

People moved to make room. The woman and her children sat down and arranged themselves around the served food.

Under his eyes, Uncle Krsto was watching the woman eat sweetly, and he finally asked, "Where were you from? I feel like I've met you before."

"I am from nowhere, poor me, since I did get to wander around through this goddamnned mountains with these two small children. I am from the Maljevich (Maljević) family from Kupinovo. We fled from Arnaut bandits. I did not want to run away initially, and I stayed with these two children to save our house so they did not set it on fire. When we saw they were burning Trpeze, I told myself that the devil was not joking with us. And since we left, the Arnauts have taken and destroyed all we had."

"God willing, you are welcome to stay with us! They are burning and killing, and nothing would help you if you stayed there," Uncle Todor muttered to himself, stuffing tobacco with his thumb into a large clay pipe attached to a long chibouk made from cherrywood.

"And where do you think you will go now with the kids?" Uncle Marko, a thoughtful old man who was ominously silent all the time except for smoking and coughing, asked the woman.

"Poor me, I do not know that. Since I found you, I would like to go where you are going, if you allow me to join. If I find people from my village somewhere down the road, I will join them."

"We see you're here now!" some cried together. "Come with us and share our destiny, whatever happens to us."

The woman smiled and humbly thanked the refugees. The children drew near to their peers to interact and play.

Someone from the camp fearfully whispered, "The Bulgarians! Watch! The Bulgarian soldiers are coming!"

Old men leaped and looked at the direction shown. Six Bulgarian soldiers with bayonets charged on the rifles and approached the refugee camp. They were obviously not coming with any noble intention. Distributed shooters spread the circle around the camp, so no one could run away into the forest.

When they came near the camp, one soldier shouted, "Sheep! Where are the sheep?"

"There they are grazing, sir," Uncle Todor fearfully responded, pointing his trembling hand toward a dozen sheep.

The Bulgarians looked at the refugees, and they began to set aside, one by one, young women and girls. "Come and stand here! You! And you and you! You will bring the sheep for us, and then we will let you go. Come on! Move!"

Four young women and two girls were helplessly trembling with their whole body, not knowing how to avoid that situation.

Uncle Krsto courageously approached the soldiers and said in a half-pleading, half-commanding voice, "There are better people to bring you the sheep if all you want are sheep. Why do you choose virgins and young women to do that for you? I will bring the sheep with children for you. Please leave the women alone. How would you like it if someone did this to your sisters and young women, as you do to ours?"

One soldier grabbed the rifle with both hands. In his full strength, he slammed the weapon butt in the chest of the old man. The old man grunted painfully on the mowed grass as he fell on the wet ground.

With open arms Uncle Todor approached the Bulgarians, but he found himself on the ground within a second, as a Bulgarian soldier hit him with a rifle. Women and children started to cry and scream, and the Bulgarians, clutching arms, dragged their victims and moved toward the house from which the chimney exuded weak, bluish smoke.

Screams and cries of women and girls who were taken away sadly echoed, ripping the morning silence off Devil's Creek. A few older women and elderly tried to go to the Bulgarians to help young women and girls, but the whistle of bullets fired from the Bulgarian rifles made them back off.

Uncle Krsto and Uncle Todor tried to stand up. A woman brought a bottle with rakiya to give to them and keep them refreshed, but both refused to accept a drink.

"I do not need it. Let me die," whispered Uncle Krsto. "Why do I need to be alive at this old age when I have to look at this evil?"

"It's better for all of us to kill ourselves when we are unable to protect our children, but we have to look at how the Bulgarian dogs dirty them," Uncle Todor was hardly able to utter.

Some of the shepherds brought sheep closer to the camp. The fog had lifted, and the sun's rays lightened the helpless country, as if it wanted to disperse evil spirits.

Suddenly the camp heard loud cries. Everyone looked in that direction. Approaching the camp and crying was seventeen-year-old Stoya, granddaughter of Uncle Marko, a well-developed, light brown girl who all living in the camp loved and appreciated for her good soul and nobility. Her flushed face was pale, scratched, and bloody. Her shirt and colorful blouse was ripped. Her lush brown hair was streaked with straw, chaff, and mud.

She was depressed and stumbling, beating her chests with her clenched fists. She was sadly whining and calling for her father Petar, who was rumored to be alive and located at Salonika Front, "Daddy, my dear daddy, where have you been? For whom do you fight? Why do you leave me alone in the jaws of the enemy? Avenge me, Daddy, and all of us who suffer like wild animals, weak and defenseless."

Coming soon were other women, all wailing, broken, and dejected. On each one was noticeable signs of struggle and violence. They were torn, scratched, and bruised in parts. Others were comforting them and said they could not do anything in that situation. But nothing could calm and comfort their broken souls and disturbed honor.

The most disturbed and depressed of all the women was Staniya. She thought of her Stevan and what he would say when he heard of the shame and embarrassment when he came back. When she saw the knife, which Vasiliye used last night to slaughter the sheep, she grabbed it. And like a she-wolf, she ran toward the house of the torture.

Many people from the camp ran to her in order to prevent her causing even greater evil. The first to come to her was Yovan, a thirteen-year-old boy.

He put his arms around her waist, saying in a pleading voice, "No, Auntie! For God's sake, enough with this all. They will kill us all!"

Others came along and surrounded her, and they took the knife out of her hands. Pale and exhausted, she slumped to the ground. Tears streamed down her pale face, and her lips trembled as if she wanted to say something. But the words could not come out of her mouth.

The injured elderly were raising themselves up and looking sadly at the scene. No comforting word could come to their minds. What would be heartening to say here? The only thing to be done was to immediately move on from that place and get as far as possible from the Bulgarian torturers.

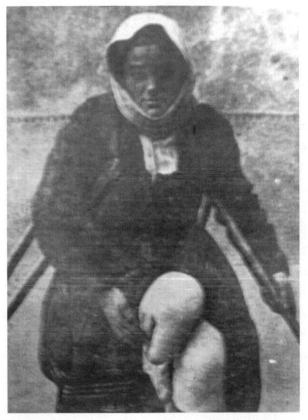

Woman in Toplica, who, as the consequence of raping and beating by the Bulgarian soldiers, lost a leg

The Hero of the Heroes

The illness of Miko Vuchinich (Miko Vučinić) prevented him from joining the other villagers in the war. He remained at home in Cat's Rock and even then when many of his neighbors went into the refugee camps.

When he was told to run away, he said, "I have nowhere to go. This is my house, and I will not leave it until it's the last breath of my life."

Miko was a man of about forty years. He was of medium height, and he had a lengthy black mustache. He did not look much different from the rest of his neighbors. He was quiet and withdrawn, but he was a brave and reliable individual, a good father and neighbor. He was one of the wealthier villagers. Although he had small children, he was with his wife, always working on the small farm field they had. He had a little bit more farm animals than others did, and this somehow seemed to present a picture in the village that he was wealthier.

After burning few houses in Trpeze, the Arnaut bandits, led by the notorious Hodzha Visoki, went in the direction of Cat's Rock. Exposed to them was Miko's house, which was glaring through the branches of orchards around it.

"Let's burn down that house!" The attacking Arnaut bandits said and headed to it.

Miko estimated the intentions of these arsonists and robbers. He had a Turkish rifle and an almost full case of ammunition placed in the solidly built basement of his home. He placed a hollow millstone over a small basement window and put the rifle through its hole. The women with children were previously sent to a shelter around Bechov Karst, in dense forest where nobody could find them.

When the Arnauts came near the house, the bandits fired a few shots from their rifles in the direction of the house. Window glass spilled, slammed, and fell in front of the basement. This was prudent to find out if the house were abandoned or not.

Miko took his first aim and fired. One of the attackers dropped his gun and collapsed to the ground without a sound. Other attackers came on, and about sixty, all seeking shelter, fell. They opened intense gunfire in the direction of the house. Obviously they did not immediately notice where Miko was shooting from, so their bullets were sent to the upper part of the house. Miko was known as a great shooter and won many shooting competitions in village festivals before the war. Such competitions were regularly held in this part of Serbia.

He again took aim and hit the second target. He heard a wild scream of a shooting bandit. Then what followed was scream after scream, a hit after hit. He listed them straight eight. Then the attackers realized that the basement had no windows on the other side of the house, and cautiously, like wild beasts, they began to switch to that side.

They noticed a stack of dry hay. Soon straw filled the house. One of the bandits lit the dry hay, and in seconds the house was aflame. The basement ceiling was on fire, and the flames fell into the basement. The smoke was pinching Miko's eyes. He coughed and choked from smoke and heat. He could not last any longer. He had obviously come to an end, but he knew his head was solid.

He opened the basement door, from which thick suffocating smoke ran out. He stood for a moment by the door and watched. He did not see anyone and walked toward the left corner of the house. Above the house he heard shouting. He peered out and saw a gathered crowd of armed men firing several shots. He heard screams, but an entire stack of the bandits' bullets quickly downed him.

Border villages of Upper Kosanica became completely empty and erupted into ruins. At night one could hear howling of hungry wolves and foxes, and at day they could hear the croaking of ravens, eagles, and vultures. Fields became uncultivated. Houses were burnt to ruins and surrounded by tall weeds. Wasteland was radiating everywhere—from the fields and forests and destroyed and burnt house ruins.

The Deserters

Refugees at Devil's Creek were preparing to extend their difficult and arduous journey. They hurriedly loaded something on their backs and other things on the two horses and donkey they had. Children were running around and minding the little livestock left, bringing them to drink from a small creek near the camp. Some of the women filled empty water bottles that the children found at the road.

Suddenly they heard sounds of firing rifles. An ammunition grain hit into the creek and threw up a spray of water. Women screamed and took the children to shelter behind the thick beech trees.

Yovan, Marko's thirteen-year-old grandson, who was a little bit away from the camp to look for a stray goat, ran until he was out of breath. Scared, he said, "I saw them. I saw two!"

"Who did you see? Speak up!?" one of the women fearfully asked.

"I saw Borisav and Mirash (Miraš) with rifles, and they are shooting."

"What, for God's sake! When our enemies leave us alone, these local thugs begin giving us trouble," said Uncle Marko sadly.

Borisav and Mirash were noticed in the forests around Cat's Rock, wandering around and wasting time. People avoided any contact with them. On several occasions they were seen stealing dairy and were known to have stolen some sheep from Kravare. They wandered through the woods and searched for things that people hid from the enemies. No one knew exactly who they were, but they were obviously military fugitives or, as Sreten once said, deserters.

They were about thirty to thirty-five years old each. They were trying to woo some young women, but the women considered them outrageously rude and refused indecent proposals. Shepherds mostly saw them and learned their names. They feared and avoided the Chetnicks, on which they were often inquiring with children.

They were especially cautious not to meet with Sreten. When they occasionally found out from shepherds that they had seen Sreten, the deserters would run somewhere in the dense woods and secretly inquire if he were still around.

The shots were coming from the northern hills range. The valley was heavily echoing with the shots, and every time a shot was heard, the sheep bounced up in fear. Deserters were shooting, wanting to create panic in the camp in order to get their hands on the sheep or anything else needed for food. Obviously they had no idea that Bulgarian soldiers were in the vicinity.

After hearing the shots, the Bulgarian soldiers ran out of the house with rifles in their hands and bowed. They grabbed shelter and moved in the direction from where the shots were heard.

The deserters did not intend to engage in battle with the far superior Bulgarian soldiers. As soon as they noticed the soldiers, they escaped into the forest. Shots from Bulgarian rifles were heard, and as they were increasingly moving further, these were heard less.

The refugees looked at each other in amazement. It seemed that no one even thought about anything at all, that is, their brains stopped and they were incapable of decision-making of any kind whatsoever. Then their eyes wandered off in the direction from where the shots were heard.

Uncle Krsto, an experienced warrior, was following the fight and immediately concluded that only the Bulgarian soldiers were firing shots, while there was no response at all from the other side. Quickly he determined that the military deserters were fleeing, giving the Bulgarians no resistance at all, and this pursuit would soon end. He decided the time had come to escape from that damn creek before the return of the Bulgarian soldiers.

"Move as quickly as possible while the Bulgarian dogs are still away!" Uncle Krsto imperiously ordered.

Women and the elderly hurried the children to gather cattle and sheep, and soon the refugees were on the move. They traveled as fast as they could. Uncle Krsto held up well and did not lag behind the others, while Uncle Todor soon collapsed. He was coughing and cursing the war, the Bulgarians, the Arnauts, and even himself.

Seeing he could not continue, Uncle Krsto ordered the item from one horse to be taken off and distributed to others and to give the horse to Uncle Todor. The old man hesitated for a long time, and he refused, saying it was not right that others suffer because of him. But eventually he accepted this help. They brought him his horse, and with an aide or large stone on the ground, he lifted up on the old wooden saddle.

Low, dark clouds were chasing and threatening with an imminent rain, but the journey continued. The terrain around the refugees expanded. The hill moved away from one another. In a difficult and painful journey, often whipped by cold rain and wind, our castaways continued on with the uncertainty and unknown, away from those damn old boundaries, fire, and humiliation. They did not think about what tomorrow would bring and if someone would give them any temporary warm place to settle and survive.

For some time, six Bulgarian soldiers were still chasing the deserters Borisav and Mirash, who fled without firing a single bullet at their pursuers. They did not care to fight. They had a completely different purpose, to survive the war alone. And if something could be profited from it, they would be well fed and drunk. But as they were the people despised and hated, the only thing left for them was to steal and rob. They were found and buried a lot of different valuable things that the people hid from the enemy before fleeing.

End of the Predators

Sreten heard of refugee movement very late. He knew they would encounter various difficulties and dangers on their way and decided to find them and be of assistance, if and when needed.

His horse trotted wearily along the narrow valley at Devil's Creek when he noticed an unquenched fire. It was clear to Sreten that, not so long ago, there was a refugee camp, as judged by numerous fresh trails of people's feet, shoes, and livestock. About three kilometers away from the camp, he located the refugees. Rifles were still echoing, but they were already pretty far away.

Uncle Krsto was very glad when he saw the horseman, whom he immediately recognized. He paused and waited for Sreten, who slowed his movement. He cordially greeted, hugged, and brotherly kissed Sreten.

Then he asked, "Where have you been, my son? Why did God not allow you to come here earlier but leave us to suffer from those Bulgarian dogs? May God judge them mercilessly."

The old man briefly told Sreten all, how the Bulgarian soldiers made them suffer as well as about the deserters and their misdeeds.

"Does this mean that Bulgarians are shooting at Borisava and Miras?" Sreten asked interestedly.

"That's right, my son, but they are no match for the Bulgarian soldiers, so they fled."

"And where did the Bulgarians come from?" asked Sreten.

"There were dogs in that house with the barn next to it. It seems they have been there for a long time."

"So that means they will return to the house when they stop chasing those robbers?"

"Sure, sure," the old man said.

"Well, Uncle, stay with God, and I will follow you for some time to make sure all is well and safe."

Sreten turned his horse and returned by the same route he had come from. When he was in the vicinity of the camp, he saw an empty wooden hut covered in high weeds. Its door was ajar, but with some accuracy, it could be concluded that human foot had not crossed that threshold for some time. He dismounted from his horse, pushed the door that then squeaked, and tied the horse to a rod from a broken window. He pulled the door and entered the house, behind which stood an old barn with a few remnants of hay and chaff.

Rye straw, which age had blackened, covered the barn. The walls were overlaid with horizontally fixed oak boards. He noticed smallish bloodstains on the primitive oak door. The house was located four to five meters away from the barn. From the north and west was built of rough stone, which was clearly seen in places where plaster had fallen away. From the east and south was plastered with mixed mud and straw. It could be seen that it was painted with white lime some time ago. Roof tiles covered it.

The small house had one little room and something else that could be a kitchen. At the north wall was a large wooden frame, made from a beech plank, for tying livestock. This spoke that this household had cattle and perhaps other farm animals some time ago.

On the west side was a window with four parts, which dirty, translucent glass covered. In the middle of the small room was a little square table with two beech benches and a rickety chair. At the corners were two wide beds of roughly shaped beech planks. An old, faded, collapsed tent material and blankets covered the straw-filled mattress. On the table was a kerosene lamp with the tip broken off its cylinder.

A typical house in Toplica in the period of the Great War

Sounds of shots from the firing guns had long since ceased to be heard. Twilight was all the stronger and had crossed into the darkness. Somewhere an owl made its first evening song, and soon after Sreten heard multiple human voices.

He hid around the corner of the barn, from where he saw six dark human silhouettes approaching the door of the house. He unhooked two defensive grenades and carefully unscrewed the lids, which he dropped into the pocket of his coat.

The soldiers opened the front door and sank into the darkness. The little room then flashed alive with a weak light of a kerosene lamp, which occasionally took refuge of shadows of human bodies to make it a little calmed down. And then the shadows disappeared. From the room Sreten could hear laughter, swearing, and rattling of portions and spoons.

Like a ghost, Sreten sneaked around the corner of the wall and peered through the small window, taking care not to be noticed. Bulgarians were sitting at a table, looking at a sizable paper map, which was on the table lying between them. Then they folded the map and began to joke about their morning's adventures with the young Serbian women and girls.

Most were teasing one with a scratched face, telling him that he wanted a girl but got a wild cat, with which he could have his eyes scratched out. To Sreten, it was clear that Stoya was that soldier's victim and she had left those marks of her fingernails. He imagined the fight between young, chaste girls and insolent Bulgarian pests.

Blood hit high in his face, and he could no longer be restrained. He struck primers of both grenades on the stone wall, kept them a little, slipped both into the room, and then jumped aside. Booming explosions erupted through the valley. The light went off, and the thick black smoke started to exit out from the window. From the room one could hear panting and sick cries, and at the end everything toned down.

For a little bit more, Sreten was standing with his rifle pointed in the direction of the door, and once he realized that the last noise in the house had ceased, he hung the rifle on his shoulder. With a lit match in one and a large revolver in the other hand, he entered the room. It was all quiet. A bunch of mutilated corpses and pieces of the table and bench lay motionless, representing a terrible picture.

He lit another match, picked up the Bulgarian soldiers' rifles and ammunition, and slowly stepped out of the house, heading for his horse. Somewhere in the distance could be heard the even chanting of an owl.

Welcome, Brothers!

Gojinovac lied on the right bank of the Toplica River. A rich Serbian village adorned the snow-white houses, often hidden by fruitful orchards. Spacious courtyards reached the river, from which they were distributed queues of old and still fertile walnut trees. The village was spread in a straight line along the wide and shallow river. Obviously each of the Gojinovac villagers wanted to have a farm accessible to the reaches of the river, and many were set there. It seemed that the villagers were happy and satisfied without much problems and the war did not endanger their lives in major way. But it only looked that way on the surface.

Locals from the village of Gojinovca received the refugees warmly and friendly. Older people were gathered together, and the newly arrived families were placed in the houses of wealthier hosts. They took care to provide food, housing, grazing of the livestock, and everything else so these mountainous, ill-fated people could feel more comfortable, rest, and forget their suffering, abandoned farms, and burnt homes.

Newcomers quickly made friends with their benefactors and, as much as possible, tried to repay for the hospitality shown to them. Children were assisting in guarding the livestock, and adults worked in the field and performed daily household tasks. There never came to any kind of strife and intolerance. It was one big, united family.

Uncle Krsto stayed at the house of young and beautiful blonde, Andyeliya (Anđelija). She was a tall and slender woman of about twenty-six years old. And above all she was generous, cheerful, and of a good character. She lived with her mother, a quiet and good old woman, and her six-year-old son. Milenko, her husband, was in the war at the Salonika Front with many of his comrades from the village of Gojinovac.

Andyeliya's mother-in-law left the house-running matters to her. Andyeliya never abused that privilege. On the contrary the young Andyeliya was a hard worker, both at home and in the farm works. She had a small but very fertile farm, which was always cultivated on time. She collected fruits and medicinal plants and fed cattle, so it was by no means noticed that a male head of the house was missing in her household.

For the refugees Andyeliya was warm and caring and did not separate them from the rest of her family in any way. Together they ate; they spent days, often joking among themselves; and handled many jobs. Miruna, daughter-in-law to Uncle Krsto, was assisting in all matters. A nine-year-old Dyoko, Miruna's son, kept cattle and helped with household work.

There was no Bulgarian army in Gojinovac, but the enemy soldiers occasionally passed through the village. They sometimes took pigs, calves, or anything else of livestock or food. Their headquarters was in the village of Shishmanovac (Šišmanovc), along with many other villages in Toplica.

One day Dyoko—together with Yovan, grandson of Uncle Marko; Staniya's Stanko; and some other children—were guarding the cattle near the village of Shishmanovac. Suddenly they noticed a man was hanging and swaying at the high gallows in the middle of the village. Frightened, they quickly led the cattle back home.

From the gates, Dyoko shouted, "Grandpa, Grandpa, where are you?"

"Here I am!" answered Uncle Krsto from the barn, where he was getting grist ready for the mill. "Here I am! What is it, my dear child?"

"Hanged men! We have seen hanged men!"

"What kind of a hanged man? What are you talking about for God's sake, my child?"

"Really! There in Shishmanovc! If you do not believe me, go and see it for yourself."

"It's nothing," interrupted Andyeliya. "Hanged people can be seen every day around Shishmanovac. But it would be better not to take cattle there. Keep it around the Toplica River instead."

Death of Lieutenant Kosta Voyinovich

Around those days the village encountered a sizable detachment of Bulgarian soldiers armed to the teeth. Two soldiers were led by a snow-white horse, which gracefully cascaded between them. The horse was saddled with a new yellow saddle, over which hung yellow leather saddle bags. In the rest of column were three horse-drawn carriages with several unarmed Bulgarian soldiers around them. They had bandages around their heads or white patches around their necks, on which were placed bandaged hands. Some were limping and had white, blood-soaked bandages around their legs.

Loads in the carts were covered with tent wings, where in parts, marks from clotted blood could be noticed. It could be concluded that the Bulgarians survived a difficult clash somewhere with Chetnicks, as there were quite a few of them in the forests of Upper Toplica, Kosanica, and Yablanica regions.

Noticing the Bulgarian column approaching the village, people were prone to houses and other buildings from where they secretly peeped and watched. When the column disappeared behind the last acacia trees toward Shishmanovac, the village came to life again.

The next day in the evening, somewhere in the village rushed eighteen-year-old Milutin, Anđelija's neighbor.

He asked a small group of people gathered, "Have you seen the Bulgarians?"

"We saw them as we see you now," answered Grozda, a young girl from the adjacent neighborhoods. "And you, have you seen them?"

"Yes, I did, and I heard certain details about them."

"What details?" asked one from the crowd. "What could you know better than we do? Maybe you were accidentally involved in a fight with them?" someone joked.

"No! But I learned something more. Have you seen that wonderful white horse with the Bulgarian soldiers?"

"We have. So what's wrong with it?"

"Do you know whose horse it was?"

"Nobody knows," was the answer.

"Well, you see you do not know, but I do," said the young boy boastfully.

"And whose is it, if you already know?" asked an anxious Grozda.

"That white horse belongs to the Commander Kosta Voyinovich (Kosta Voinović), who died yesterday at village of Grgure near Blace in the fight with the Bulgarians. Kosta and several of his Chetnicks died there. How many, no one knows, but it's thought that many Bulgarian soldiers died as well. A man from Donya Konjusha (Donja Konjuša) told me that the covered wagon was carrying perished Bulgarian soldiers. There were over ten times more wounded soldiers as well."

Kosta Voyinovich (Kosta Vojinović), the commander
of the Ibar-Kopaonik Chetnick detachments

"How it came to the battle, do you know?" the husky voice Uncle Vuyo (Vujo) from Cat's Rock somehow asked.

"They say a woman was bringing food to Chetnicks in two large baskets on a yoke. They say her son was with the Chetnicks. Bulgarian patrols have noted that and were following her. When one of Chetnicks came out before the woman to take the basket with food, the Bulgarian patrol returned and informed their command. Luckily someone has informed the Chetnicks, and on the arrival of the Bulgarian army, they decided to ambush the soldiers.

"Kosta deployed his people into an ambush and positioned a machine gun in the middle. The clash was brief but very intense.

Bulgarians were numerically and technically superior, and slowly they began to surround the Chetnicks. Seeing that the enemy surrounded them, Kosta Voyinovich ordered that the Bulgarian siege must be broken, even at the cost of their lives. The Chetnicks rushed, sweeping all before them while the Bulgarians repositioned, unable to keep off the onslaught of the Chetnicks. Fighters were dying on both sides. Kosta, riding on a white horse, was encouraging and braving his compatriots, but hostile grain hit him straight to the head, and he silently fell. The horse was standing beside the dead master, and the Bulgarian soldiers who surrounded Kosta's body seized it. Others saved themselves by escaping the siege."

"And did Kosta Pechanac participate in this struggle?" the curious Uncle Krsto asked.

"No! He was not there; nor does anyone know where he was."

"May God curse him where he's hiding just when he should be fighting the Bulgarian dogs," Uncle Krsto muttered sullenly, sorely squeezing a piece of tobacco into his big pipe made of red clay.

Insurgent group of Kosta Voyinovich at Kopaonik Mountain

Stoya Darling, Cheer Up!

Gojinovac plunged in the first winter snow. Livestock were placed in warm barns and pens, and the shepherds drew in their homes, occasionally taking to the street to play with snowballs and again seek warm rooms soon after that.

Often gatherings were held in sheltered houses, which young and old equally well attended. Older people were talking about the war, asking about their family members at the Salonika Front. They discussed events in the country and the atrocities of the Bulgarians. In addition sometimes there were a few glasses of rakiya, after which people became more relaxed and brave. They were often assigning someone to guard and observation duty, while the others would dance with the sounds of flutes and sing Serbian patriotic songs.

The youth was united and in no way different from each other, even that one belonged to the mountain and the other to the plains. Everyone was cheerful and often forgot about that war, especially at such gatherings. Only Stoya was always sad. All the efforts of her mother Yelica (Jelica) to somehow cheer her remained unsuccessful.

Yelica would often say, "Stoya sweetheart, go with your friends to gatherings and cheer up. You are still very young. If you do not go out anywhere, you will remain closed in yourself as an old woman. What will the neighbors say about your bad attitude?"

"What am I to do there, Mother? I am the most unfortunate creature in the world, so it's better not to get involved with honorable girls."

"You are not right, Stoya. No, you cannot complain about anything! What happened was a force that could happen to anyone. Who is the one who could be saved, if they were found in your situation on that unfortunate day at Devil's Creek? There is no such person in this world."

"There are some like that, Mother. Did you forget Pava, Radoye's wife?"

"Yes, Pava, but where is she today? It's true she honestly lost her life, but she is dead."

"I wish I were dead. Today they would all praise and respect me. In this way I am left to live as despised and shunned."

"None despise or avoid you. You alone are avoiding others, and that will not bring any good. Do you see that you are so pale? If you continue this way, soon you will meet your own end."

"All I know and see, Mother, but I cannot do otherwise. My youth is buried, along with the joy and happiness with it."

Her mother was no longer touched on this topic. She saw it all in vain, so she left her to her fate.

Masho Is Alive!

Andyeliya often wrote to her husband at the Salonika Front, and she occasionally received letters from him. She wrote extensively about the refugees, mentioning their names and the names of their family members who were believed to be alive and located on the Salonika Front. She asked about them. She wrote about Pava and everything else she knew. She described the case of violence of the Bulgarian soldiers at Devil's Creek, mentioning Sreten and his heroic deeds as well as deserters Borisav and Mirash and their looting of abandoned and burnt villages.

One day at Andyeliya's house came the old village head Stoysha (Stojša). In his hand was a letter with the red cross on the envelope. When a letter with the red cross arrived in the village, all of those who had soldiers on the front line would hurry to inquire whether the letter perhaps mentioned the name of their family members.

Andyeliya never read the letter in front of the audience, but she was happy to briefly communicate the contents of the letter, omitting of course what could personally concern her. She finished elementary school and two years after that. She knew how to read fluently and clearly and then present what would be interesting for the people present there.

Andyeliya entered a nicely furnished small bedroom and closed the door. She leaned on a small round table, opened the letter, and began to read it carefully. She read it once, squeezed it against her chest, kept it there for a few seconds, and then again continued to read. Once she finished, she packed the letter in an envelope and placed it on the table. Then she went out and found Miruna in the barn, where she was working something around cattle.

Then she asked, "What are you doing, Miruna?"

"Tending to the livestock," replied Miruna.

"When you finish, come and talk with me."

"Wait. I'm almost done with all my work. I will be with you in a few seconds."

Two women sat facing each other in the kitchen. There was a brief silence for a minute.

And then Andyeliya said, "I called you to tell you that I received a letter from Milenko."

"Well, good for you, Andyeliya. At least you know that your Milenko is alive and well. I have nothing on my Masho," interrupted Miruna.

"If you do not know anything about your husband, I know," said Andyeliya with a smile.

"What can you possibly know? You are in a mood to joke with me?" worriedly noted Miruna. But she was not able to hide her curiosity.

"I'm not kidding, Miruna, but I am seriously saying that your Masho is alive and well. Now if you know how to read, I'll show you what my Milenko wrote to me about Masho."

Miruna wept. When she calmed down, she said, "I am not literate. I always had to stay and work at home and could not go to school. It was a few hours to travel to the nearest school from my village, and we girls sat at home, looked after the livestock, and attended to other work required."

Andyeliya read the part from the letter that referred to Masho. Miruna was full of happiness, and she quickly ran to find Uncle Krsto to tell him everything Andyeliya read from the letter. The old man imagined for a moment and then removed a Serbian cap off his head with his arm. Two happy tears slowly rolled down his wrinkled face.

Finally he said, "I always knew that our Masho would not leave us nor let us down. Thanks to the good God, he will soon again be with us. Do not you worry about him, my daughter! But tell me again what he said. Did you read all that from the letter?"

"From the letter, Dad! Exactly as he wrote. He said to us that Masho would write now that he knows where we are."

"He will, God willing. I know our Masho."

Death of Uncle Todor

That winter Uncle Todor ended up being very sick. After receiving a hit of a rifle butt from the Bulgarians at Devil's Creek, he constantly complained of chest pain. He somehow kept encouraged until recently. Mariya, although aged, was running around him like a young woman, prepared food and drink for him, massaged him, and cooked tea from herbs she collected in the mountains over the last summer. But nothing helped. The sickness was taking momentum, and by the early winter, the old man fell to bed.

One day someone said to Mariya that a woman in Kondzelj (Kondžell) was able to treat and remove a variety of illnesses. She should bring something of personal belongings or the patient's clothing and not be afraid or worried about anything.

Mariya called her daughter-in-law Miluna and said, "Dear child, get ready and go to Kondzelj to the house of Ljubica, the healer. You know they told me that only she can help my Todor."

She found scissors they used for sheep shearing, and from the old man's woolen pants, she cut off a few small pieces of strings and rubbed them slightly between her thumb and index finger to make a small ball, which she gave Miluna. "Here's this stuff for you to give to Ljubica. She knows why it's needed."

"I will go, Mother, when you say, but I do not believe those fortune-tellers and healers. You'd better inquire if there is any doctor around here. I know it takes money, but we could sell one sheep and pay for the doctor."

"What kind of doctor? Are you crazy? I am told that no doctor can be compared to Ljubica and her powers. Now go, as I say, and do not worry about anything."

"I will, Mother. Do not worry. May God help us to find him the cure."

She put on some old broken clothes, dirtied her face a little with ashes to look unattractive to any Bulgarian soldiers she might meet on her way to Kondzelj, and moved on.

Ljubica's small house was on the edge of the village. It had no fence around it. Under the eaves were hanging bundles of some sort of grass. There were white mallow, yarrow, mint, parsley, vitalion, and a host of other kinds of plants. There were no other buildings than her homes, and this showed that it was a very poor household.

Miluna approached a small, cracked door, knocked twice on it by hand, and pushed it open. She immediately saw a woman of dark complexion who was a little bit overweight. She was about forty years old. She wore a wide and long skirt and blouse tight to her body. For Miluna it was not difficult to conclude who the person she saw in front of her was, so she immediately felt sorry she came in, but she had no other options because of the expectations of her mother-in-law.

"God help you," stammered Miluna somehow without a will.

"May God give you all the best, my sister. Come in. Do not be afraid!" greeted the healer who was not getting up from a small, three-legged stool.

Miluna entered and sat down at the bench and against the wall to rest.

"What goods bring you here, my sister?" Ljubica wanted to know.

"It's not good, I swear to God, since I am here," replied Miluna quietly.

"It'll be all right, my sister. It will be fine. You just tell me what hurts you."

"Nothing hurts me at all, but my father-in-law is very sick."

"God forbid, my sister. God forbid. But have you brought something from him?"

"I brought it, if it's good." Miluna started to open a bundle tied by the corners of her scarf. "Here's a ball of woolen threads from his clothes!" She handed the bundle to Ljubica with threads of Uncle Todor's old trousers.

"And the rest? Money I need, my sister. Without money he cannot be treated."

"And how much is needed?" asked Miluna.

"A little money, my sister. Only one dinar for you. Nothing more."

A silver dinar was valuable, but if she did not finish the job, it would be something her mother-in-law Mariya would never forgive her for. Miluna had guarded—or rather hid—some silver dinars in a small pocket in the inner side of her clothes, just in case they were needed for emergency. She turned her back to Ljubica, loosened her clothes from where her money was tied up, took a dinar, and handed it to the woman in front of her.

"Here, now give me the cure!"

"Wait, my sister. First I need to do some reading of the past. Throw a penny (para) in this ball, and let's see what it says."

Miluna again loosened her clothes, found a penny, and then placed it in the clay bowl. Then Ljubica poured water and placed pieces of Uncle Todor's clothes in it. Then with old, rusty tongs, Ljubica lifted a piece of lit charcoal and placed it in a bowl with water. The charcoal released a squeaking noise and, when saturated with water, fell to the bottom of the bowl.

Ljubica cried, "It seems, my sister … it seems, hmmm? Someone threw black magic on your father-in-law. He is poisoned with black magic, but do not be scared." She again put the lit charcoal into the water. "You see. I told you he is poisoned. Get him to drink this water on an empty stomach three times a day so he will be as healthy as a newborn again."

Ljubica's medication did not help, and Uncle Todor died after ten days. He was buried in the village cemetery in Gojinovac, although his life's wish was to be buried in the cemetery near his Kravarsko village in the Upper Kosanica.

Radoye, Your Pava Is Dead

Milenko had long been hiding the news about Pava's death from Radoye. Although his Andyeliya wrote about it extensively, it was hard for him to tell Radoye. This was like a large weight that pressed his simple soul. He loved Radoye and appreciated his manliness, courage, and kindness to subordinates, but he knew how much pain it would inflict if he knew this, as he loved Pava more than his own life. But every secret must come to an end. Milenko one day decided that the long-kept secret finally must be announced to Radoye.

It was one Sunday afternoon. Life went as usual, full of boredom and uncertainty. Soldiers were staying comfortable and resting, and several officers gathered to play a game of cards.

*Serbian soldiers on the Salonika Front (Captain
Nikola Ilic from Nish with his comrades)*

Radoye was carried away while looking at some newspapers. Who knew how old the edition they were from? He decided to read it from beginning to the end.

Suddenly Milenko's voice startled him. "Sergeant, sir! I have something to tell you, but it's hard to start because I know this news will affect your heart. But what must be must be because I believe it's not humane that I am still hiding this from you."

Radoye lowered the paper and looked at Milenko. He did not know what to ask him because he assumed it was not any kind of good news. He finally said, "Speak, Milenko, no matter what it is!"

It seemed, for Milenko this time, it was harder on his soul than Radoye. In a husky voice he said, "Your Pava is dead." Barely audible Milenko pronounced, "It's very hard for me to introduce you to this sad news, but I had no other choice."

Pale as death in the face, Radoye asked, "You said, my Pava? How do you know my Pava?"

"I do not know—nor have I ever known her—but unfortunately this is still true. She died honorably. Bulgarian degenerates and thugs killed her. I have not told you that your people from Cat's Rock have found refuge in my village of Gojinovc. If I told you that, I would have to say to you all I know. So I kept quiet until now, but it's no longer possible to stay this way.

"Back in late October, they arrived at my Gojinovac, fleeing the Arnauts who were burning your village and looting everything they found. Your people are distributed in families around Gojinovac, and at my house we have Uncle Krsto, father of our Masho. About their acceptance by us and other details, my wife immediately wrote to me upon their arrival. About the death of your wife, my Andyeliya wrote lengthily to me, along with the events in Devil's Creek, the death of Kosta Voyinovich, and other details. She wrote to me about the Chetnick hero Sreten, who fiercely avenged the death of your wife and the other atrocities of Bulgarian soldiers at Devils's Creek and elsewhere."

While Milenko spoke, Radoye silently swallowed every word, and although it seemed that his thoughts were absent, they wandered around the forests around his home village, cliffs of Devil's Creek, and who knew where else. He smoked one cigarette after another. His throat was dry, and some currents, until then unknown, were circulating every part of his body.

He felt fatigue and weariness. He collapsed on wet and blackened stubble. His facial muscles danced as if in a spasm. Long he lay down and thought, bringing a variety of decisions, which he later realized were impossible. He thought of revenge. He sought ways to switch to Toplica and join Sreten to organize an uprising.

But soon he concluded that all this was impossible. He was an officer, and it would soon come a day when he and all his company would move to a common revenge. He knew that this difficult war not only destroyed his Pava but many letters brought unbounded sadness to many of his brothers-in-arms.

And they all eagerly awaited vengeance as much as he did.

Letter from Masho

Days around that time in Gojinovac passed uniformly bleak. Various news circulated through the village: the hanging of strangers in Shishmanovac, where the Bulgarians often invited Serbian people to recognize the unfortunates; the hunger and poverty in the villages of Lower Kosanica and Yablanica; the Bulgarian atrocities against defenseless people; and many other terrible stories.

Winter was somehow quickly fading. The snow was melting, and the Toplica River often immersed parts of the fertile farmland. Parents had to constantly look after young children so they would not run down to the river.

One afternoon the old village head Stoysha (Stojsa) appeared with a letter in his hand. At his call, Andyeliya excitedly ran to invite him into the house. "Come on, old man!"

"God help you!" greeted Stoysha.

"God bless you, sir. Come in. Come in. You're not in front of an enemy's house." As she spoke, Andyeliya did not take her eyes off the letters in Stoysha's right hand.

"I will come in since you are inviting me. Is this letter for any of your people? I would not say it's from your Milenko."

Andyeliya grabbed the letter and looked at the address. When she pushed the old man into the house, she ran to the basement, where Miruna was processing some wool for making clothes.

From the threshold Andyeliya cried, "Hey, Miruna, it looks like you'll have to buy me a present! Will you quickly tell me until I change my mind and go away?" As she spoke, her hands held the letter, which was behind her back so Miruna could not see it.

Miruna stood up and began to remove the wool off her clothes. Her eyes shone, and her cheeks filled with blood. A soft smile lit up her face. She intently watched Andyeliya to find out if she were telling the truth. She knew well this beautiful woman and was convinced she was not prone to any stupid jokes. Then she noted that Andyeliya was holding her hands behind her back, which gave her more hope.

Finally she said, "I will, no matter what you have to say to me."

"Well, if you want, look at this." Andyeliya showed the letter and then gave it to Miruna. "Here! It's yours, Miruna!"

With trembling hands Miruna accepted the letter and started to look at it curiously. She saw something in the text and noticed a red cross, but she could detect nothing else. Finally, she asked Andyeliya, "Open it, Sis, and say from who it is."

"I know already who wrote it for you," Andyeliya mischievously responded. "Your Masho wrote that letter from the front line!"

"You are cheating me?" Miruna quickly pulled the letter from Andyeliya's hand, and her cheeks became even redder.

Andyeliya silently watched this innocuous being. She was like a great child, whose joy was fully manifested in the expression on her face. She felt sorry for teasing her any longer. "Go find Uncle Krsto and Dyoko, and ask them to come to me together to read you the letter."

Uncle Krsto was sitting on a small tripod stool and slicing a wad of tobacco. With a piece of a pencil, Dyoko carefully wrote letters that Andyeliya taught him at some stage.

Even from the door, Miruna cried, "Letter, Dad! We received a letter!"

"What letter? From whom?" the old man, surprised, asked.

"Look at it!"

"From whom? Speak!?"

"From his father! From him!"

Miruna never referred to Masho by his name, and Uncle Krsto was clear whose letter that was. He slowly rose, leaned against his hand on the floor, and stared at his daughter-in-law.

"Oh, what's wrong with you today? I hope you have not eaten any wild poisonous mushrooms."

"I did not, Dad, but let me give it to Andyeliya to read the letter for us. Come here, Dyoko, my dear child."

Still with some disbelief, the old man followed his daughter-in-law and grandson. Andyeliya carefully opened the envelope. The letter, written by untrained hand, was presented on all four sides of the two-folded sheet of paper.

She began to read aloud. The old man listened, pulling the thick fumes from a large clay pipe while Miruna was hiding that she was wiping tears with the corner of her headscarf. The room was deadly silent, which only undermined Andyeliya's voice. When she finished she closed the letter, placed it in the envelope, and then gave it to Miruna.

Although she read it slowly and carefully and they all listened to it from the beginning to the end, Uncle Krsto asked Andyeliya, "In God's name, Andyeliya, what does it say? Will he come back home soon?"

"He will, old man, when the time comes, but we will have to wait a little bit longer."

"Thank the good God that they are alive and well, and when they do come, we will always welcome them with full strength of our hearts. Thank you, Andyeliya, when you blessed us with this conversation and cheered our sorrow souls. Now we know he is alive and continues to be with God. Go boil some coffee from barley, and let's have a drink with Andyeliya. May God give her everything she wishes."

"Slowly, slowly, old man. Some real coffee is at my place. Also we can have a glass of rakiya as well. I know it will suit you right now at this moment."

"It will, thanks to the good God, now or never, but it's a shame we always drink at your place and never at our home," the old man replied.

Andyeliya just now noticed that the old man Stoysha vanished while they were busy with reading the letter. She brought three glasses and a bottle, which held over half of the yellowish alcohol beverage.

Then she filled a glass and toasted, "My dear old man, thanks to merciful God that soon we will be even more delighted and see our dear soldiers, healthy and happy."

She drank half the glass and then passed the toast to Uncle Krsto and Miruna.

The Bulgarian Machine Gun

The enemy's positions at the Salonika Front were located close to Serbs troops. Actually they faced each other, both well solidified. For a long time, there was no heavy fighting, but it was not fully quiet and calm. Occasional skirmishes between the Serb and Bulgarian armies were making the situation such that every soldier knew where he belonged to. The enemy was in front of him, and he had to be patient and survive to the end.

Along with other allies, the French Allied army were building the momentum and planning, and it seemed there would be a major clash at the front line at any moment. Soldiers had to keep aware with wide-open eyes over the situation so they could never fully relax and get comfortable. Thus they were constantly on alert and under tension. All were eagerly expecting the decisive moment that the offensive should decide the fate of that damned war.

A heavy Bulgarian machine gun was grossly infringing upon that little bit of silence there at the front line. It was enough that the enemy noticed a single soldier out of a shelter and/or a trench, and hives of long, hellish bursts of the machine gun fire would erupt. There had been attempts to silence it, but these did not work so far.

Serbian infantry in position at the Salonika Front

Radoyc, an infantry sergeant, and Petar, his neighbor from Cat's Rock, were sitting in the trench and softly speaking.

"What about you, Petar? Can you stand that damned Bulgarian machine gun? How long have we been listening to it so far? It does not allow us to calmly think, let alone rest in peace, take a nap, or something."

"I do not know, Radoye, but if someone asked me, it would not be for long before it makes that noise, no matter what happens to me. I had enough of that Bulgarian dog who gave me so much grief in my miserable life. You've heard of Stoya's case, the situation of our dear others at Devil's Creek, and the case of your poor Pava? Are these crimes to remain unpunished, and are we to let it not be avenged by our own hands? It could be said that Sreten's revenge is sufficient, as he killed the executioners. But Sreten did not get a chance to avenge all the evil that the Bulgarians have committed to all our people around Toplica and other parts of our poor country. This tells us that we must find an opportunity to do something with our own hands so those bastards realize we know how to retaliate and their misdeeds cannot remain unpunished."

"You're right, Petar! I hold the same opinion. Revenge must be, and I think that's true!"

"Easy, Radoye," interrupted Petar. "Let's silence that nasty Bulgarian machine gun and start our revenge right here and now. If we survive, we'll know we've done something. And if we die, we will do so honorably, like Serb people, soldiers, and patriots."

"That is not a bad suggestion, Petar, and I fully agree with you. I have also been wondering how to get that machine gun silenced forever! I'm going to talk with Major Protich (Protić), and I believe he will agree and release us for this action."

The terrain between the front lines was ravaged by numerous artillery shells and covered by few stunted bushes. It was about two hours after midnight. Small drizzle was coming from the dark clouds and made the dark night even murkier. The heavy Bulgarian machine gun occasionally fired and then silenced. And it resurfaced after a few minutes. Besides the machine guns, the front was quiet, and no other shots were disturbing the piece of that dull night.

The two men were quietly and silently penetrating through rare, stunted shrubs, bypassing many ruins caused by artillery shells. The target of their movement was the heavy Bulgarian machine gun nest. They were armed with revolvers, bombs, and other weapons they did not have or else they would be noticed. They wore thick woolen socks and no shoes.

A dense eclipse was forcing them to move closer to each other so they would not get lost in the dark, as it could be very dangerous in this case.

"Closer, Petar. Closer," whispered Radoye to exhort his companion.

"I'm here. Do not worry," responded Petar, barely audible.

The Bulgarian machine gun released a few short bursts. A beam of bullets hummed over the heads of the two companions, but experienced warriors easily concluded they were not noticed. It was clear to them that they were already quite close to the machine gun nest, so they increased alertness.

From the machine gun nest, they had not heard any human voices, so they could conclude that the other crew had fallen asleep and only the gunner was awake.

A few meters forward, Radoye and Petar were clearly hearing the snoring of people who were deep asleep. They were very close. Crawling silently they stopped their breathing. They were already in front of the enemy and could see the silhouettes of the heavy machine gun and the gunner behind piles of stacked rocks, which seemed to hide them from the enemy. As if by command, with both of their hands, they activated defensive grenades against the stones, waited a tick of time, and then threw them into the darkness toward their final target.

The earth shook the powerful explosions, which seemed even more terrible in the still of the night. Two human figures came rolling down the steep terrain between the fronts, and soon they were heading toward the Serbian trenches. Major Protich had informed his soldiers about the action that Petar and Radoye performed, and they smoothly jumped into the trench.

The enemy was confused and surprised. They heard voices and swearing of Bulgarian troops. Soon after a fierce fire, not surprisingly, caused no damage to the Serbian side.

The heavy Bulgarian machine gun and its crew never again disturbed the silence of the night at the front line. Revenge was apparent. Two warriors, with less sorrow in their hearts, were waiting for the outcome of that severe and intolerable war.

Stoya, Do You Love Me?

The spring of 1918 arrived, somehow before its usual time. Farm work was already widely performed, and the fields became full of farmers. Fruit trees blossomed like they had not for a long time before.

The Bulgarian soldiers somehow appeared very nervous. They hung their heads down and did not look like themselves, torturers and bullies as they were until recently.

People from Gojinovac carried agricultural work jointly. Gathered were youth and women, and still they worked hard together as there was no tomorrow and so on until they finished all the work required. At such joint work, they felt less fatigue, and workers were joking and having fun. Sometimes an occasional quiet little song could be heard.

Andyeliya's farm fields were located mostly near the village and the Toplica River. Farm work gathered all the youth. The youth from Cat's Rock were mixed with the adolescents from Gojinovac. Only occasionally could younger women be observed. One was happy to receive jokes and completely fit the social context around her. Youth, when they performed field work, felt somewhat more comfortable and freer if adults were not present, and they were happy to receive all the burden of field work, of course except for mowing and plowing, which adults performed.

The sun raised by a whole spear height, and a good part of the field work was completed. The farmworkers were already noticeably tired, but they continued further without any special vibrancy.

Stoya and Radosh (Radoš), an eighteen-year-old young man from Gojinovac, were moving further away from other workers. Between them was a conversation in which the others were not participating or paying attention to.

"What is the matter with you, Stoya? You constantly somehow stay put and do not interact with us. Do you not like the company? Or maybe you're so silent by nature. When I was watching you, I was convinced that I was facing a cheerful person. But somehow it's a hard word to draw from you. I have been watching you from the first day of your arrival here, but to be honest, I did not have the courage to approach you, so here, even today, I hardly dare to do so."

Radosh was the son of a wealthy rural family. His father Trifun was an honest and respectable farmer, at whose home was placed a largest refugee family. Although he was the only child in the family, Radosh was hardworking and good-natured. Tall and well-built, he looked more like an athlete than an ordinary farmer. The Serbo-Bulgarian War found him in the third grade, lower in high school, when he dropped out to work on his father's farm.

As soon as the refugees arrived in the village, he noticed Stoya, whom he liked at first sight. She was a slender, blonde girl from the mountains that had appeared to him as someone rarely encountered. Her sky-blue eyes were deep and betrayed love and warmth, along with gentleness and goodness. It was just the way in what was shown in every fraction of her body, in every movement and procedure.

For a moment Stoja looked at the boy and said in a low voice, "I like the company of people, but I am trying to keep aside. I am just an ordinary village girl. I am even in a worse position than the others."

"I cannot understand how and why you would say that, Stoya. To me, you are the most beautiful and best of all the girls I know. When I think you will go someday, I wish this war would extend indefinitely so I could watch you and admire you much longer."

"Radosh, you are overreacting. Or maybe you are making fun of me and trying to hurt my already wounded heart that will never heal."

"Now it all makes sense," said Radosh sadly. "So you have a boyfriend who you expect to come back from the war. You need to tell me immediately so I do not bother you any longer."

"You are mistaken, Radosh. I do not have a boyfriend; nor have I ever had one. But there is something else, something that has darkened my entire future and killed my will to live. It made me such that, as you said, keep retreated and closed to myself. Do not ask me what it is because I will not tell you, as I abhor it myself. I despise myself. So please do not ever say a single word about any of my beauty or goodness. Rather despise me because I deserve it."

"Halt!" interrupted Radosh. "From the first day I saw you, you came to my heart. I'm dreaming about you in my heart, but I never had the courage to approach you because of your eternally sad look and posture. This winter I wandered around the village gatherings to look for you, but you were never there. I was thinking what was wrong with you. I inquired and inquired. A long time there was nothing I could detect, which made me even more troubled and worried. I finally found out everything that happened in Devil's Creek, everything that made you unhappy and why you are separated from socializing with young people. On hearing of that fatal accident, you became dearer to me, better known and clearer, because of what had befallen on you. Such tragedy could only kill the soul of a noble and honorable person such as you are."

"Thank you, Radosh, when you think about me. It's true that my soul is broken and it would never recover. I'm sorry you like me. Maybe you had some serious intent, but I will never marry. This is why I say that to you. It does not matter how much you really love me. Soon you will forget me and meet better girls than me."

"I do not ask for a better girl, Stoya. I'll never ask for one as long as I can see you, even if it's up to the end of my life."

"Do not do that, Radosh. You do not know what others and your family will say when they hear about the misfortune that has befallen me. They certainly would never agree for me to be their daughter-in-law."

"All they know, as well as I do, and they do not complain. On the contrary they have the best opinion of you. They like you as much as I do and would be happy if you married me."

Somehow Miruna appeared with breakfast, and they all moved to the shade of a large oak tree.

Since that day everyone could notice big changes in Stoya. She became cheerful and talked much more, and her face got a pleasant freshness and blush.

One day while Stoya weeded the field near the Toplica River, Staniya came with two buckets full with laundry on a yoke across her shoulders.

When she saw Stoya there, she stopped near her, put the laundry on the grass, and asked, "What are you doing, Stoya?"

"I started clearing this garden of weeds, Staniya."

"Fine, fine. I know you are a hardworking girl."

"Are you kidding me, Staniya? I am not so valuable, but something must be done."

"Did you see Radosh passing by?" Staniya asked with a cheeky smile on her face.

"I did not see him," she answered calmly, but her face blushed.

"I know you rarely see him; however, I am just asking if by chance you have seen him."

Stoya did not respond to Staniya's teasing.

"Handsome young man ... and it seems to happen that he likes you."

Stoya ignored this question and left it unanswered. She felt somehow uncomfortable. She was even more amazed why Staniya knew about her relationship with her Radosh since they held it in strict secrecy.

"Sorry to bother you, Stoya, but I've talked with Radosh about you because I was asked."

"Who asked, Staniya?"

"Actually it was Radosh and his mother. His mother said her son would love to marry you, and she asked me to speak with you.

You know me, and I think you and I have the confidence to tell me everything."

"I have faith in you, Staniya, and I can tell you that I like Radosh. But it's not the time to think about that now. When the war is over, there will be an opportunity for that."

"Yes, we are at war but still have to think about it. Just because it's war, it might be important. After all, think about it and give me the answer once you can."

Staniya turned and headed toward the house. Stoya remained confused, thinking about all of this that had happened. Maybe she should not have admitted it to Stanija. Maybe it should have been kept secret until the end of the war. What would happen if Staniya talked throughout the village all she knew about her and Radosh?

On the eve of St. Vitus Day, it was raining heavily. The Toplica River blurred and slightly rose, but very little. In the morning on that St. Vitus Day, Radosh prepared bait and a fishing rod and went to the Toplica River to fish. Tall grass, soaked by rain and dew, was wetting his trousers to above his knees, but this did not bother him. Fishing was his thing, and no other sport could replace it for him. Ever since he was eight years of age, he had a fishing rod, and he was the best fisherman in his village. Catching fish by a net, hands, or in any other way did not interest him. These methods were disgusting and unsporting for him. Radosh loved to observe how the float played at the water's surface, and when it dived, it was a real pleasant experience for him.

That morning Radosh picked a fishing spot over a deep vortex and began to prepare the hook. Suddenly behind him he heard a deep male voice, "There you are, dude. I have been looking for you for a long time, and finally I found you at the most desirable place. Now before I make a hamburger out of you, tell me. Whose girlfriend are you trying to flirt with?"

Radosh, whose thoughts floated on the surface of the deep vortex, startled this sudden voice from behind. When he turned, surprised, he saw Ostoya (Ostoja), known bully and rural troublemaker from Gojinovac.

Ostoya was a year or two older than Radosh was. He was slim and had a bit of an unusual elongated neck, so people in the village usually called him Roda (stork). By nature he was blunt and assertive, which often provoked fights, from which he was usually on the receiving end of beatings. The villagers hated and avoided him, and they never called him to help with the farm work.

"Hey, Roda, what forces you to the river at this morning dawn?" asked a calm Radosh.

"Do not play like you do not know anything. You know very well what brought me here! Tell me whose girlfriend you are cheating on and approaching!?"

"What kind of girlfriend, Roda? Since when do you have a girl, and who is that lucky person?" Radosh asked.

"Well, since you want to know, my girlfriend has been Stoya, and if I see you try to talk with her, you will have to deal with me. Do you understand!?"

Radosh dropped a hook out of his hand, and his blood welled in his face. He thought, "Stoya with Roda, that rude, silly person? For him to take away the girl of my dreams? Is it possible that she is so sneaky and dishonest? No, it cannot be! It was a lie that must be punished immediately."

He turned to Ostoya and said in a sustained voice, "Now what, Roda? Do you want for me to give you Stoya? Is that your final wish, or do you have something more to say?" Radosh asked.

"Why are you asking me this? Maybe you want her, dude?" Ostoja clenched his fists.

"Not only do I want her, but she has been my girlfriend. Now clean out from here before I flatten you down!" said Radosh angrily.

"Well since you want it, here you go!" said Ostoja furiously and swung his fist. But he did not manage to put it down before Radosh's heavy right fist welcomed and bounced him back.

Ostoya stumbled but quickly lifted and jumped toward Radosh, swinging his fist and saying, "Wait! Now you will see who you're dealing with!" His torrential momentum did not score the right goal because Radosh jumped aside and Ostoya flew past him.

Radosh grabbed him by his shoulder, turned him around, and lightning-slammed his fist on Ostoya's chin. Ostoya fell flattened near the riverbank. Radosh grabbed him by his chest and lifted him up. A new punch was rushing at Ostoya's cheekbone. After which, blood flew off his nose.

"Have you had enough, big bully?" asked Radosh, standing straight over Ostoya, who was lying there without moving.

Radosh raised his fishing rod, placed bait on the hook, threw his line away into the water, and placed the rod on the ground. After a few minutes, Ostoya slowly lifted, blew his nose full of blood, and retreated back to the village.

When he had moved away about ten meters, he turned his head and said, "We will meet again, you son of a bitch. Just wait!"

"I'm waiting for you, Roda. Do not worry. I am available for you anytime. Only the next time, I will not be so gentle with you," Radosh said quietly and lifted the fishing road off the ground.

Just as Ostoya disappeared behind the first house, Radosh rolled the fishing line, threw baits into the whirlpool, and moved to the village. Although he held that Stoya was proud and had strong character, he believed and was convinced that she loved him. But there was some doubt and something that was bothering him.

He found Stoya in the garden behind the house, doing something around the flowers. Once he saw her, he gave her hand a sign to come to him.

With a smile on her face, Stoya approached him. But when she saw his scowling face, she was worried and asked, "What, Radosh? Did something happen that caused you to look like this?"

"For sure something happened to me, and you would have to know what could happen."

"I do not understand what's going on. What would I have to know?"

"I'm asking you, Stoya, and I want a straight answer from you about what you have with Roda and why I do not know about your relationships with him."

"What kind of roda, and what kind of relations?" asked a surprised Stoya.

"Ostoya! That kind of roda. Are you going to tell me you do not know him?"

"I know Ostoya well. What about him? Are you saying that I'm in love with him?"

Radosh was comforted with these words from Stoya. He calmed down and said in a gentle voice, "Listen and halt! Earlier I got into a fight with Roda because of you."

"Because of me?" interrupted Stoya, puzzled.

"Yes, because of you. He says you're his girlfriend."

Stoya started to think a bit about all kinds of things. Her thoughts wandered to the past, from the day of arrival in Gojinovac until that moment, but she could not remember that she ever had any conversation with Ostoya whatsoever. She remembered he had once long watched her while she was working in the garden, but there was not a word.

Finally she said, "I cannot shut anyone's mouth, but I'm sure this guy and I did not speak even a single word. If he said I were his girlfriend, he's crazy or just wanted to provoke a fight with you. Well, that's all I can tell you, and you probably know enough."

"I know you, Stoya, and I believe you. And I know that idiot Roda! I know he is a liar and plotter, but I will handle him differently from now on."

"Radosh, I think there should be more confidence and trust between us. You should not believe anyone's stories because tales will exist as long there are vicious people in the world."

Radosh looked around to see if anyone were watching, and once he was satisfied that no one was around, he put his arm over her shoulder and gently said to her, "Stoya, sorry for being so rude and suspicious, my darling. You really do not deserve this."

He removed his hand from her shoulder and, slightly smiling, went home.

The Bulgarian Call

It was the peak of the summer. Curtains of heated air were created above the roofs of houses, and sheep were grouped tightly side by side, keeping their heads down to the ground, breathing heavily while hiding in shade of an old oak three. The Toplica River was full of children who were screaming, playing, cooling in the water, and splashing water one over another. On village roads were squeaking carts overloaded with the grain harvest. Thirsty chicken were overheated and wandered yards looking for some water and shade. At one house a dog stuck out its tongue from which saliva was dripping. Swarms of annoying flies, like a flock of satellites, circled around its head.

Somehow someone in the village suddenly drummed a drum. The children ran out of the river and onto the street. Adults left their work. Those with carts stopped for a moment. All the people alive came and surrounded the drummer.

When he saw a sizable pile of people around him, the drummer stopped drumming, pulled out a paper from his pocket, and began to read, pausing after each new word. "Guys, hear ye. Hear ye! The Bulgarian military command orders that all adults, both men and women alive, should urgently report before the military command in Shishmanovac for important announcements. Any person who does not obey the command will face strict measures."

"Come on. Tell us, Tadiya. What is it? We hope it's not some kind of ploy set up by the Bulgarians?" someone from the crowd asked.

"I do not know! I do not know, people, and it's not my business to know."

The drummer hung the drum on his side, bent the paper, stuffed it in his pocket, and went to announce the command to the other end of the village.

Such orders were not unusual for the villages, but whenever they heard the drum in the village, something would poke their hearts and cause stress. They knew their occupier was not hosting any good intentions, so they always thought what this new command might expect from them and what surprise awaited them in Shishmanovac.

Even after the departure of the drummer, the people stood there transfixed for some time. Bulls were waving their tails and defending themselves from flies that were attacking their eyes on the hot sunny day. The willingness to work was subsiding in the people because of the uncertainty about their destiny.

"What if they do something to us?" Vasiliye anxiously asked, directing the question more at himself than at others.

"We'll see," said someone from the crowd.

"Certainly they do not call us to eat and drink with them," said the other.

"There is nothing here to guess," noted one old man from somewhere with his deep voice. "They called us, and we have to go. We do not want to think and speculate before we find out."

Men and women gathered to collectively go to Shishmanovac. Somehow it seemed to be safer when more people were in the crowd. Therefore when they gathered together, all went silent, like they were at a funeral. It was clear how miserable and sad it felt to lose freedom, be enslaved and suffer under the occupier, and be subjugated and humiliated in that way.

Internment of Serbian women and elderly

Shishmanovac was some two to three kilometers away from Gojinovac, but the sad crowd needed quite some time to cross that short distance. Nobody was saying anything. It seemed that they were not thinking of anything at all, although every one of them was, deep down, thinking about sad and dark things.

When at last the group reached the vicinity of the village of Shishmanovac, they saw a group of people gathered in front of the Bulgarian military command. The people were silent and mired in their own thoughts and sufferings, staring at the large double gate in front of which was an armed group of frowning and banal Bulgarian soldiers, standing around and expecting new arrivals. The people from Gojinovac hurried and mixed with the others from the neighboring villages. There were quiet whispers, inquiries, and sighs. No one knew the real reason for the call.

Suddenly the double door of the Bulgarian command swung open. Armed Bulgarian soldiers pierced through the crowd of the people and set them against the wall of the building with rifles at ready to shoot position and raised bayonets. Through the open door came eight Bulgarian soldiers. Four were carrying two stretchers with people covered with old army blankets. Two to three meters in front of the gates, they stopped and stripped off the blankets. People saw two human corpses, bloodied and disfigured. One was very young. He could have been barely twenty-five years old. Blond hair was soaked with blood in places. His suit was made of peasant cloth, quite worn but still standing. He was wearing old military boots.

Another corpse was a little older, maybe by about ten years. The unshaven person was tall and skinny with dark hair. He had a long, black mustache, and his long, black hair was tangled and unkempt. He was dressed in a suit of peasant cloth, worn out that had been patched at the knees and elbows. Black, clotted blood covered his pectorals. Swarm of flies buzzed over the bodies, every now and again descending on the bloody spots of the dead men.

The interpreter translated the command of the Bulgarian officers, "People, you are invited to identify these bandits and give us their names and other information. Anyone who happens to know them and does not tell the Bulgarian military authorities everything he knows about them will be strictly punished. Each of you is bound to take a good look and recognize these bandits. Those who recognize the bandits and provide the Bulgarian authorities with requested data will be financially rewarded. Now you all come forward and take a good look."

The people become disturbed. Fearfully they began to approach the dead human bodies and were silently praying for them. Sheltered by the masses of the people, an old woman was using the end of her scarves to wipe the tears that rolled down her wrinkled face. However cries could not be heard. The rest held broken and grieved hearts somewhere in the depths of their chests.

Men and women passed and looked. They finally stopped by the Bulgarian soldiers to hear the new command.

When all had looked, the interpreter translated, "Come on, folks. If you do recognize these bandits, freely enter the command and disclose everything you know about them to the commander. You will immediately receive the credit you deserve."

Among the crowd there was dead silence. Nobody set aside to enter the Bulgarian military command.

"Come on, folks. Feel free," said the interpreter. "Mr. Lieutenant is waiting and seeking the truth. I said what will happen to those who know something but keep silent. It's therefore in your interest not to remain silent but to tell us what you know about these bandits."

Even after these words, the people remained quiet and motionless, while the Bulgarian soldiers were becoming more and more irritated. Finally the officer angrily began to scold and threaten how they would retaliate to the bandits at their houses as well as to those who were in the forest. The commander selected four strong, old men and ordered them to dig a hole in which to bury the bandits. And with harsh curses, they ordered the other people to disperse and go home.

No one present recognized the killed Serbian men, even as the old lady with scarves continued to wipe her tears in front of the Bulgarian military command. Only after several days did the villagers from Gojinovac hear that the Bulgarians went to burn some villages in Upper Yablanica, and there, Sreten and his small group of Chetnicks ambushed them. The Chetnicks allowed Bulgarian soldiers to enter into a small canyon and then opened fire at them from all sides. The sudden attack caught the soldiers by surprise, but they quickly pulled themselves together and returned fire.

A dozen Bulgarian soldiers fell from the first volleys of bullets. Then the fierce battle opened. For some time the canyon and nearby gorge echoed of gunfire and explosions of grenades. Husky and well-sheltered Chetnicks offered tough resistance to the far superior enemy. However the Bulgarian soldiers applied a stratagem, surrounded the Chetnicks, and discovered their shelters. Sreten ordered them to break through the enemy line, but two of his mortally wounded comrades were left on the battlefield.

The Bulgarian army abandoned the burning of villages on that day and returned, bringing along their own casualties and the two dead Chetnicks.

Wedding Celebration

Radosh and Stoya were standing by the edge of the Toplica River, sheltered from the views of people and houses by high and thick locust trees. Radosh held her in his arms. She, blushing up to her ears, lowered her gaze and looked at the tips of her opanaks (traditional Serbian shoes made of leather with curved tips at the front end).

"You have to choose one, Stoya. Time passes, and we stand at an impasse. I cannot stand like this any longer, and you must decide," Radosh said in a low voice.

"I know this, Radosh, and it's difficult for me also to decide. You love me today, and tomorrow when you start to complain about my unhappy past, you will be tired. Then you will send me back to where I came from. Well, that's why I'm afraid and reluctant."

"Stoya, we spent the entire spring and summer together, and here it's already autumn, but you still do not know me well. You think I would not be able to choose a girl from our village, but you must know that, since I met you, you adhered to my heart as no other girl ever."

He grabbed her head with both of his hands and pressed his lips to hers in a long kiss. She was not defensive. Her face was burning by some sort of strange fervor. She was drunk on something, which she had never felt in her young life before, drunk with the first true love.

Finally she gently broke away from his embrace and said, "I love you, Radosh. And each day more and more, I love you. I feel I can no longer live without you. But what does your family think about me?"

"My love, Stoya, they would be happy for you to be their daughter-in-law. I've already talked to them, and they cannot wait a moment to see you at our home."

"I agree, Radosh, to marry with you, no matter what happens later!"

Again their lips closed together, and her arms were thrown around Radosh's neck for the first time.

It was Sunday, sometime in the first half of the month of September 1918, in the Trifun's house. People were gathered around long tables, and everyone was drinking and partying. Under the wedding veil was Stoya, who held onto the arm of a tall guy with a long white towel over his shoulder and a gilded buxus tree twig on the lapel of his short coat.

No loud singing and music were heard, although all the youths from the Gojinovac were present. No man could make Trifun sit down. He was running around the house, ordering the servants and making sure that food and drinks were served in front of each guest, no one skipped a glass of rakiya or any other food, and beverages were made available especially for the occasion. The people were happily yelling, toasting to each other, and joyfully congratulating their host.

Trifun suddenly exclaimed, "Brothers and friends! Today, my son, my only son, is getting married to a beautiful Stoya, and this is my first joy of this kind ever. I know we are at war and it's not the best time for marriage and celebration, but still the children have fallen in love, so let them be happy."

"God bless them!" interrupted voices of others.

"I made sure," exclaimed Trifun, "that no one disturbs our celebration or surprises or upsets us in any other way. That's why I assigned a team of young guys to monitor and guard around my house so no one spoils our fun. I cannot let my first joy go silent, and I call upon all of you to sing and celebrate in the way that our ancestors did in the past at the time of freedom. Come on in good health, my brothers, and let us happily and healthily welcome our brothers and sons from the front line and soon celebrate the end of the damn Bulgarian power and this war."

"Good luck! Good luck!" guests already warmed by alcohol beverages cried in a loud voice.

Someone started a song, and others joined in, quietly at first and then much louder later on.

Fall my brothers; spill your blood.
Throw yourself into water and mud.
Leave your village; let it burn in flames.
Remove from us slavery and shame.

A young man with a flute skillfully played Serbian folk dancing tunes. Looking for fun and dancing, boys and girls quickly formed a dancing circle, and soon most of the adults and elderly joined in.

Joy lasted late into the night, and then when all got quiet without fuss and songs, the guests withdrew to their homes.

So beautiful, blonde Stoya, the tall and quiet girl from Cat's Rock, who previously lost all hope and willingness to live, became a permanent resident of the sweet Toplica village of Gojinovac, despite all the misfortunes and sufferings of hers in that difficult and bloody war.

Although Trifun tried during his son Radosh's marriage celebration to satisfy everyone, to ensure that everyone was well fed and drunk, wagging tongues were still making conclusions of their own.

One evening near the Toplica River, Radosava and Petra, two women from Gojinovac who came to wash clothes there, began a conversation about Radosh and Stoya.

"Did you go to the celebration at the Trifun's family, Petra? Such wedding and celebration has not been seen in our region before."

"Yes, Sis, I did. Well, I went to see how the things were in such a wealthy home and what else."

"Well, my sister, what a celebration they made, like it's not a war but peace."

"I swear to God. For him this is not war but a real peace. Nor does he have anyone in the war. Nor is he waiting for anyone of his to return from the front line. Even the Bulgarians somewhat avoid his house and do not bother him."

"It's easy for him, my sister. His house is full of everything, and he gives a bottle of rakiya, a good lunch, or a good dinner to anyone who ever comes to his house. And you know what people are like? Bribe them and then do not worry about anything."

"That's right for God's sake. There he is healthy and fat, while my husband and your Nedya (Neđa) are rotting somewhere in trenches at the front line … if they are alive. But even that we do not know."

"Well, at least they could have taken a good girl rather than that Bulgarian slut. Why did God curse us by sending her here? It could be some of our own honest girls to be made happy with their wealth," Radosava said, referring to her daughter Milka, a little backward girl.

"Well, my Radosava, it's hard for an honest girl to find good fortune. It's easy for that humbug girl who knows well, like a fox, to twinkle and twist around a guy and make him crazy about her so he cannot notice any better girl."

No one knew for how long these two tabbies were to continue nagging, unless somehow old farmworker Kosta approached and spoiled that wonderful conversation.

Return of the Refugees

With the Bulgarian troops, they noticed major changes from day to day. Somehow they became concerned, less aggressive, and more withdrawn into themselves. Shepherds were the first to observe that and were freely passing their cattle around Shishmanovac. One day shepherds saw that there were no gallows in Shishmanovac. They notified the elders, who then interpreted each in their own way how they understood this manifest.

Some thought the Bulgarians wanted to show their lack of interest so they could take on the people easier, that is, to relax them and, in that way, get their bandits from the forest. Others thought the enemy wanted to deceive people to peacefulness, to relax and loosen up, which would thus reduce vigilance and make it easier to get to their hidden assets, which would then become an easy prey for the Bulgarians. However the people were mostly convinced that the end had arrived for the Bulgarian occupiers and they were not much long to roam around their beautiful country.

Everyone talked widely about how Chetnicks in Yablanica and Kosanica were increasingly attacking the Bulgarian patrols and outposts and the Bulgarians were therefore withdrawing to the larger settlements in Toplica.

Sometime in mid-September 1918, the sun was still sending warm rays over the countryside, and the people were mingling in the fields to soon finish all required farm work. Refugees, grateful for the warm and cordial dealings with their hosts, attempted to return the favor as much as possible, so they spared no effort to assist them in all matters. So each refugee family participated in all common work. Old people were usually working in gardens or yards, mostly light work.

In the evening, when people withdrew from the field work, Uncle Krsto called his grandson Dyoka and said to him, "Go from house to house where the people from Cat's Rock are staying, and tell them that all are to immediately come to me, along with their hosts, to discuss an important matter. Do not forget any of the houses. You know very well where they all are staying?"

"I know, Grandfather. First I'm going to call my aunt Stana and uncle Vasiliye and then my grandfather Marko and …"

"Oh, do not try to spell out one by one, but just call all. You hear? Everyone! Now go!" ordered Uncle Krsto.

The boy obediently ran and disappeared around the corner of the first house next door. A little later, a small group of men and women gathered at Andyeliya's home. Andyeliya presented a bottle of rakiya and served all of them.

When Uncle Krsto found they all had come, he calmly stood up from the small tripod chair on which he was sitting, coughed, and then said, "I called you all to agree on one thing, which I hope all of you will support."

"Let's hear it!" Uncle Marko was first to call.

"I think," continued Uncle Krsto, "the time has arrived to slowly go to our loved homes. As I see it, the Bulgarians will no longer roam around our region, and the Arnauts burned and robbed all what they wanted and could, so now they all do not have what to loot and take. But what is most important is that the rest of us leave the honest people who truly brotherly received and helped us all this time to deal with their affairs in their own space. I invited you here to speak your view and, if you agree, to determine the day in the name of God for us to go back to our homes."

This speech surprised Andyeliya, who served rakiya. "My dear old man, we are not tired of you, and as far it concerns us, you should not hurry to go back. Here, we work together, we operate as a family, and we think it's not difficult for either of us. And yet we have become friends, and we are closer than we have ever been before. Please stay with us this winter, and you can go back in the spring when the weather improves, God willing. I know your countryside is calling you and your land lies fallow and abandoned, but you should not go there until we have the Bulgarians in our country. I would like to ask you again: What happens if they trouble you again on the way?"

"Thank you, Andyeliya, and all of you for fraternal and selfless acceptance and warm shelter," noted Uncle Marko. "But what is enough is enough. It's the right thing that we welcome our dearest at home, if God permits, when they return from the war. Our homes were burnt down, but we will rebuild them. Our fields were abandoned, robbed, and remain fallow. We will renew them, and everything will be back as it was before. That's why we need to go as soon as possible, as long as this nice weather remains for now."

"I'm good to go!" concluded Vasiliye. "There is nothing more to wait, and I would suggest we wait only for another day and go the day after tomorrow. Until then we can prepare our poor people, and we will have more time to rebuild something on our lands and raise a little roof over our heads."

"Yes, that's right!" the others agreed. "We leave the day after tomorrow, early in the morning."

The fraternal villagers of Gojinovac gave a heartbreaking farewell to the refugees. Once the villagers learned of their preparations for departure, a burden all fell on the souls, which they themselves could not explain. For a long time, they all lived in harmony, performed together all works, and shared joy and sorrow together. This could not be forgotten in a single wipe. Youth, who usually spent time together, worked in the fields, and participated in gatherings and the rare dance parties, were merged into one soul and accustomed to one another's company. Saying good-bye was set to leave deep marks on their souls.

Older people from Gojinovac planned some kind of departure ceremony. The night before the departure of the refugees, they were both sad and happy. At the Trifun's house, long tables were arranged, where all, both locals and refugees, sat down. Glasses of drinks were flying around, and warm meals were evaporating. Toasts were called, and declarations of wishes and gratitude were heard. A youth with a flute played Serbian dance music, and all refugees, full of sorrow and sighing, danced their last dance in Gojinovac.

The day of departure was quiet and sunny. In front of Andyeliya's home, a crowd of people gathered. Everything was ready to go. Gojinovac's women brought various presents and stocks such as bags of wool, beans, dried meat, flour, bottles of rakiya, and a lot of other stuff that they could get for the refugees. Many of these women were sad with tearful faces, each complaining about parting with the poor but honest mountain people, and they were concerned about their fate and adversity. Each woman from Gojinovac knew that her friends were soon to encounter sad, burned ruins of their houses. As much as possible, they did not spare any effort to prepare food and other necessities for the refugees to take.

Stoya was sobbing in tears. This return of her people to Cat's Rock felt like a heavy load on her soul, as if she had never thought this day would arrive.

Trifun, her father-in-law, approached her and was trying to comfort her with gentle words. "You have no reason to cry, my daughter. As soon as the first opportunity arises, I will send you together with Radosh to spend a few days with your family there. When the war is over, you'll have a chance to go there more often, and yours will surely come to us regularly."

Stoya, after these words and promises, became calmed a little. She was looking forward to the day when Radosh would see her birthplace and she would be able to walk with him those same mountain paths in Kosanica, which she so willingly walked and were so dear and sentimental to her.

The War Is Over, Grandpa!

Cat's Rock and adjacent villages were looking very sad: burnt ruins overgrown with high weeds, remains of houses, abandoned fields, and roads overgrown with grass. It could barely be recognized that people were ever living there.

The refugees, emotionally broken up, each in his or her own desolation, were so sad to watch the ruins of the former houses. Women were quietly crying, small children were asking about it, and men were thinking what to do next and where and how to store the few remaining livestock and families. No, there was not enough time to think.

They began to work as soon as possible. They found old rusty axes and some other tools, and work began. Part of the preparation was done in Gojinovac. They purchased nails, hinges for doors and windows, locks, and other stuff most needed to start. People from Gojinovac gave them lots of essential things, as they knew it would be very difficult for them to obtain such material in their area.

Everywhere in the woods could be heard sounds of axes. Women were on their shoulders pulling material, and here and there, a horse or a cow was used to transport everything that could not be carried on one's back. For timber there was no problem because the high mountains were full of trees.

For a short time, the people lifted up a little roof over their heads. It was not like before, but it provided adequate shelter from rain and the storm, and soon they became somehow happier at their own places, independent and free. It's undisputed that the villagers from

Gojinovac were pleasant to them, and they tried to make them feel at home all the time. They had to eat and drink; however, they had always felt like subordinates and strangers. The Bulgarian soldiers did not appear anywhere, and neither did the Arnauts cross the old border any more.

Somewhere on the last day of September, a man approached near Uncle Krsto's hut. Uncle Krsto was doing some work in front of the hut, and when he saw the stranger, he put down the axe and sat to rest.

When the man got closer, he greeted Uncle Krsto, "May God help you, old, honorable man."

"May God give you all the best. Come sit down and relax a bit."

"Okay, when you say it, I have traveled for a long time, and now I'm so tired."

After asking each other about their health, Uncle Krsto asked, "And where in God's name are you going? Here, since we returned from Toplica, our people saw not a man or even the Bulgarians."

"I am coming from Ivan Tower, and I am going to Vaseelyevac to visit a friend, if he has returned from the refugees. But since you mention the Bulgarians, I hope we will never ever look at another one again, God willing!"

"What are you saying, my friend?" asked Uncle Krsto.

"That's what I heard. The Bulgarians are doomed, and we will not even look at another one here unless he is our prisoner. They laid down their arms and fled to Bulgaria. Our boys with the help of the French army and other allies broke the enemy's line of resistance at the Salonika Front. And now the enemies are beaten and retreating quickly. Well, I'm telling you this, and you feel free to talk to whoever you want about this further."

The old man turned to the hut and cried, "Miruna! Miruna!" Miruna came out. He told her, "Look for that bottle of rakiya, and get it here."

Miruna disappeared into the hut and quickly returned with a bottle of brandy. She greeted the man and returned to the hut.

When they finished two or three glasses of rakiya each, the passenger stood up, said good-bye to Uncle Krsto, and went. When he disappeared behind the first forest trees, the old man went up to Bechov Karst and began to call, "Heeeey, Marko! Heeeey, Marko!"

In front of Marko's house, his grandson Yovan answered, "Who's calling?!"

"Hey, tell Marko to immediately come to me and ask him to bring along Vasiliye and others as well."

"Okay, good, good!"

From Uncle Krsto's hut to Marko's was a good half-hour walk, but the clean mountain air and throats of the highlanders enabled clear and well-understood communication. After an hour, standing in front of Uncle Krsto's hut, a few older men, women, and children gathered. As they arrived separately, those who arrived first were led into a conversation about everyday tasks and problems.

And when all were assembled, Uncle Krsto took some official position and began to talk, "I called you to tell you a story that will make you all happy, and it's one we all have been looking forward to for so long."

"I hope you, Uncle, always have good news," inserted a curious Staniya. "Come on. Continue! We are all listening to you!"

"Shortly before a man came from Ivan Tower and stayed a little bit with me. We had a glass or two of rakiya. He told me that our troops and allies broke the Salonika front line and are now chasing the enemies. He said the Bulgarians laid down their arms and fled and we will no longer look at them in Kosanica, Toplica, or anywhere else in Serbia."

"Oh, someone was joking with you, Uncle Krsto?" responded Uncle Marko with disbelief. "If it were not kind of a spy or some saboteur?"

"No, my brother Marko. What kind of spy? That's our man from Ivan Tower. You can see that the Bulgarians are not coming. We cannot even see a single one."

"Well, if so, get up everybody, and let's go right to my house now. There will be more of that rakiya I bought from Gojinovac, and I should have something for a snack!" joyfully exclaimed Uncle Marko.

Uncle Marko's proposal was accepted, and everyone started to move along the steep walking path toward his home. From his belt, Vasiliye pulled out a rusty handgun, lifted it above his head, and began to pull the trigger. Heard were three clicking and two shots, which encouraged participants, and a song begun to boom.

The children came running to the roadside from their huts, women were suspiciously peeping, and the song went on.

Where Are You Now, Bulgarians?

From day to day, Sreten's detachment grew more and more technical and numeric. Increasingly frequent attacks on the Bulgarian were bringing the benefits of weapons and war material.

Already reduced number of the Bulgarians in the villages across Kosanica, Yablanica, and upper Toplica were a constant target of Chetnicks, especially Sreten's squad, who were appearing everywhere when none was expected. Brave, experienced, and a good strategist, Sreten knew when and how to attack and surprise the enemy. He and his squad were a nightmare for the Bulgarians, who never felt calm and confident anymore that they would not be suddenly attacked. Therefore they began abruptly to abandon smaller settlements and withdrew to the larger centers, towns, and cities.

Without any wind to stir it, the rain was calmly drizzling from the thick, low clouds. Although it was dawn, any chirping of birds or howling of a hungry wolf, which were plenty in that area, could not be heard. Only two ominous ravens were disturbing the morning silence, croaking somewhere above the tops of high beech trees, searching for a place to rest bedraggled wings.

Right and left of the gorge, a muddy mountain road was winding, poking the rocks between high beech trees. The rocks were aligned along the width of fifty meters, extending from the road to the ridge of the mountain on both sides. Behind every rock could be seen the barrel of rifles and some human heads with broad folk hats or black fur hats, down upon which poured rainwater. Barrels of rifles and human heads were turned in the direction from which the mountain road was coming.

Sreten was sitting somewhere in the middle of his group, and his sharp eyes were looking at the gorge in front of him. When he was satisfied that nothing disturbed the morning silence and no one was around, he got up and softly began to instruct his soldiers that no one fire a bullet until he heard his command. He had issued some orders. Then he returned to his spot and took on an ambush. Heard were whispers about the rain, which mercilessly was making them wet.

"This rain decided to bathe us, and if someone is resolved to travel to hell, he does not have to be washed before the trip."

"If I'm going to hell, do not bathe me. I will go in tar anyway," said an old man in a low voice.

Sreten had all his attention focused on the cliff, as if someone were whispering about the arrival of the Bulgarians. He jumped up, turned to his fighters, and cried in a soft voice, "Silence! They are coming. Roll over and be quiet!"

There was an undertone transfer of commands. "Quiet! They are coming."

Sreten noted that the two ravens were frightened and rose rapidly by flapping wings and then flying over his fighters. Then his sharp ears reached dampened footsteps of many people. Soon they heard the people's voices, laughter, and curses.

Fighters of Yablanica Chetnick detachments

Soon a group of armed men appeared and marched through the mud without any order in a crowd, such as an armed mob without command and military discipline. It may be noted that they felt carefree and in complete safety. There could have been about sixty of them. In the front of the column, there was a young, swarthy officer with two noncommissioned officers, and on his sides were two soldiers with machine guns.

It was barely raining with cold water falling upon them. It seemed it was going to stop at any moment. Day had arrived although the dawn was just passing. Suddenly a burst of sharp and short command was heard.

"Fire!"

A loud, deadly salvo, mixed with human screams and cries, filled the gorge to the top. Bluish smoke created a transparent curtain between the enemy lines but did not make a barrier for the rain of bullets, which were bringing vigilante revenge to the paralyzed Bulgarian ranks.

The surviving enemy soldiers, beheaded decimated and afraid, did not try to give much resistance but attempted to escape. However according to the established plan ahead, Sreten's fighters were quicker and cut them from retreating. Broken in small groups at the last minute, they tried to resist, but soon shots of Sreten's fighters calmed them.

The nameless canyon above Yablanica had long served as a rich source of food for many eagles, vultures, ravens, wolves, foxes, and other carnivores and scavengers until the villagers discovered it and buried remains of the Bulgarian soldiers into a common pit.

Bulgarians never dared to seek the lost squad. It seemed they did not have time because they were all trying to save their own lives and soon leave this bloody and vicious avenger's country.

Here Are Our Dear Soldiers!

A snow-white carpet covered Cat's Rock, and small houses and huts thrown across the hills resembled a kind of giant mushroom. Not a soul was outside. Everyone was locked up, like a silkworm larvae in its nest. Even dogs did not bark or roosters did not crow, and it all gave the impression that it was abandoned and a deserted place, awaiting spring when new life was to be revived to the villagers.

Only the night came alive in this seemingly enchanted village. Eager to talk and have some entertainment, the people gathered in the evenings at someone's hefty log hut, where they most often played the ring game. They were split in two, numerically equal groups, facing each other. They put a blanket across the table, and ten hats, caps, or woolen gloves were distributed across. Someone had to hide a ring under one of the hats or gloves, and the opposing party was to locate it. If they found it, they would get ten points. Otherwise the opposing group would get that many points that were left untouched.

They often spent a good part of the nights listening to a skilled minstrel who sang popular heroic and patriotic poetry about medieval battles of the Serbs against the Turks and heroes including Milosh Obilich (Miloš Obilić), Marko Kraljevich (Marko Kraljević), and others. A man named Vukoye Vasilyevich (Vukoje Vasiljević) composed a song about the heroic death of Miko Vucinich, so this song lately was the most popular with the people.

On one wintry afternoon, a man appeared from the Kravarsko cemetery on a beautiful white horse saddled with a new state saddle. The broad-shouldered man was young and strong. He was of medium height with strong male features. He was wearing a long overcoat, on which were gleaming new epaulettes with one star on each. His officer's cap covered thick, black hair, beneath which glowed two large, black eyes. His black and small mustache gave his face even greater charm, beauty, and masculinity. On his new leather boots easily rattled sharp, nickel-plated spurs. On the left side of his overcoat peeped the hilt of a sword.

Although this young man had a nice and firm face, his black eyes were concealing immense sadness. It was not difficult to note that this burly guy suffered immense pain for quite some time and his young soul carried a pressure load, below which, in spite of his gigantic strength, was not able to break free.

Once stepping on this soil, his pain was strengthened. He knew he would never see those beautiful black eyes or luscious lips and receive a kiss of a woman with whom on that same path they often passed, whispering sweet words to each other. He knew those beautiful eyes and luscious lips, belonging to his great love, whom he jealously guarded from anyone during her life, was now hidden right there close to him, buried under the black, harsh earth.

On the white horse, he moved toward Cat Rock's cemetery. Once he arrived there, he alighted. And after tying the horse to a fence, he took off his cap and started to walk in easy steps around primitively built monuments.

His eyes wandered from one to another monument. The snow cover did not allow him to find the fresh grave easily. Suddenly his eyes rested on a beech cross, where faded letters written by a clumsy hand read, "Here lies the body of Pava, one who honorably died at the hands of damned forever enemies."

Two stone tears, like a vanguard, fell down the brown and tanned face. And immediately after them was a flood of tears rushing one after another. He stood still. He seemed not to cry, but those big, black eyes turned into two inexhaustible sources of tears. He did not speak. Even his lips were not shifting, but still something inside him was quietly speaking. These were his consciousness and his memories.

Under that small cross and the sad pile of snow, he was seeing his young and beautiful Pava, that swarthy girl with black ponytails down her lush breasts who proudly walked at gatherings and festivals at Becho's Church. He remembered how many boys, including himself, were longingly looking and following that glorious and proud girl, but all were only daring to approach her. He remembered their first conversation in which, due to his excitement, he found it difficult to find words to say to her. He recalled the first heart-shaped cake he stretched to her with his trembling hand and the white veil over her head. Ah, how her wonderful face, framed in black, luxuriant hair, glistened under that white veil. He remembered their sad parting when he had to hug a rifle and go with his brothers to the war in defense of the homeland.

He was silent as a statue. He could not see or hear anything. All his thoughts were concentrated on the wooden cross and pile of snow in front of it. He saw only the past, memories, and sadness. The neighing of his strong white horse startled him out of his reverie, and he returned to reality. He glanced around and just wondered where he was. He went to a wooden cross and kissed it. Then he went to the white horse, loosened the reins from a fence, and threw himself into the saddle.

The horseman first saw his mother Tominka, who was feeding cattle in front of the hut. Puzzled and frightened, she paused. With the sudden appearance of an unknown soldier in the twilight days, she did not say anything.

Suddenly she turned, and in an elderly voice, she called out, "Stanko! Stanko! Come out here for a while!"

Stanko appeared in the doorway of the hut and asked, "What has happened?"

"Here is someone coming to our house, and see if he is not a Bulgarian."

Stanko put his left hand over his eyes to obstruct the sunlight and looked in the direction of where Tominka was showing. Then in a low voice, he said, "It's not Bulgarian. It's a Serbian officer. I see him and his epaulettes."

The horseman was slowly approaching. The officer's hat was pulled over his forehead, and it was not easy to identify who he might be. When he arrived at the house, he dismounted from his horse, put the reins over his left arm, and said, "Good evening!"

"God bless you, sir," Stanko replied, not taking his eyes off the stranger.

"You forgot me so quickly, Uncle Stanko? Have I changed so much in these few years?"

To Tominka, the voice of this young man could not remain unknown, even after so many years. She spread her trembling hands, which closed around the strong officer's neck and said, "My son Radoye, my dearest. Since when your mother has not seen you?"

Torrent of tears prevented this old woman from fully expressing all her joy. She was silently holding her hands clasped around the neck of her beloved child until Stanko separated them so he could welcome his dear nephew. Radoye lost his father early in his life. He considered Stanko to be his father. Stanko, with all his warm heart and care for Radoye, deserved such respect.

After entering the hut, they long discussed Pava's death, and Tominka spoke of her virtues, her kindness to everyone, and especially compassion to her mother-in-law. While talking about Pava, Tominka choked with tears. She had no female child of her own, and Pava was her daughter and daughter-in-law at the same time.

The villagers soon learned that Radoye had arrived, and people rushed to see him, some even to inquire about their own relatives. Soon old men, women, and children filled the little wooden hut. They all gazed at Radoye, listening to his every word, and the children were screening him with their eyes from his head to toe. They stared at the epaulettes, sword, boots, and spurs. They observed the cap with the Serbian insignia (Kokarda), and every one of them wanted to be like him, "just like Radoye."

Women admired him and whispered among themselves.

"Oh, poor Pava, if she were now alive just to see her Radoye here," whispered Staniya.

"Well, she would be so happy to see such a man," whispered Yelica. "He was handsome before, but now even more. No mother could be prouder for such a son."

"Who will be the lucky one to marry him? But I think no such women in our region could replace Pava to him," noted Milusha and sighed.

"There will be one like that. If not in our region, somewhere else for sure. Men's mourning passes quickly, just like a creek when overflowing. So it will pass him too," said Staniya.

Cold and snowy days were passing. Three days after Radoye's arrival, Masho came back. Uncle Krsto's joy was extraordinary when he saw his only son. Once he looked at him, tears of joy covered his face.

"Well, my own blood, my hawk, I knew you would come back to us. I know my Masho. Let no man talk about him otherwise," said Uncle Krsto cheerfully.

Miruna was skillfully hiding her joy. In front of her father-in-law and son, she avoided every encounter with Masho, but once Uncle Krsto went somewhere with Dyoko, she would place her arms around his neck.

From the first day, Dyoko was somehow shy of encounters with his father. If his grandfather and his mother left the house and he stayed with Masho, he would quickly find a reason to run out of the house, not to be left alone with his father. It seemed strange and unknown to him. Masho, still in the early days of his return, noticed Dyoko was avoiding him, so he tried in many ways to come closer to him.

One day Masho decided to go to Koorshoomliya to buy something, so he called Dyoko and said to him, "Son, tomorrow you and I will go to Koorshoomliya, and I'll buy you something nice."

"Will Grandpa come with us?" asked Dyoko curiously.

"No, Son. Grandfather is old and not really able to walk long distances. You and I are young, and we can."

"What about Mom? She is young."

"Mom is young, but she has to stay with Grandpa. Would you leave him alone?"

"My grandfather, God bless him, is not old. Only he is a little weak ever since the Bulgarian in Devil's Creek hit him with a butt of a rifle. But he's still going well. You should have seen how he was marching when we were returning from Gojinovac. Probably better than you could."

"Good, Son. Good. Your grandfather is going well, but he has to stay home for something to do. You and I need to go to Koorshoomliya."

"Well, if I have to, I will," replied Dyoko unhappily.

In Koorshoomliya, Masho bought Dyoko's outfit of a black yawl, a wooden scrap board with chalk, a piece of sponge tied to its frame, and all sorts of other little things.

"Here's your wooden scrap board. I will teach you to write, and you will go to school in the fall." Masho passed the scrap board to Dyoko.

Dyoko grabbed the board and dragged the chalk across it. Once he saw the white line, he screamed cheerfully, "Dad, this is drawing!"

"Yes, my son! You will see how your daddy will teach you to write, and you're going to be the best pupil in the school."

"And I will become an officer like Uncle Radoye?"

"You will, my son, if you're good and if you learn well."

From that day nobody could separate Dyoko from his father. His mother and grandfather were amazed at how suddenly so much friendship between them developed, when, just yesterday, Dyoko was fleeing from Masho, like he was a total stranger.

"A child is like a puppy, my daughter. If you give him a bit of food, he'll run to you all the time."

"That's true, Dad. He cannot separate from Masho now."

"No, Daughter. The child should love his father. He loves us. He has just seen more of us in these days, like he learned to run around us."

A few more days passed, and then Petar came home. On that day Ruzha had kept cattle near the house of Makochevich's (Makočević) family, and once she saw the man in uniform, she was afraid and hid herself behind a bush to look at where the stranger would go from there. The man walking on the path appeared somehow familiar, so she had a better look at him from behind the cover.

Once the man walked past her and turned his back, Ruzha jumped from behind the cover, rushing to him and crying, "Dad, my dear, is that you?"

Obviously surprised, the man abruptly turned away. Seeing the girl that jumped into his arms, he asked in amazement, "Ruzha, my child, my love, how you've grown! Daddy would not recognize that it was you unless you spoke, my dearest." He hugged her in his arms and held her for so long to hide the tears that were welling from his eyes.

Arriving home Petar told Staniya that Stevan remained in Nish and would come home in the next few days. He deliberately avoided saying that Stevan, while chasing the enemy army, was wounded slightly and remained in Nish in the hospital for treatment.

Staniya sensed that something was wrong with Stevan, and one day she went to see Milusha and Vasiliye and ask them to look after her house and children. "You know, Milusha, I have to go to Nish. Something tells me that something happened to Stevan. I had a dream the other night that he came home so angry about something, and he was not talking to me. I was bugging him with all sorts of things to trigger conversation, but he kept silent. Therefore I have to go look for him, to see what happened to him and find out why he did not come home like the others."

"It's far, Staniya, and Nish is a big city, so it would be hard to find him. It would be better to ask Petar to give you some more detailed information about him rather than you wander alone so far via remote roads."

While Staniya and Milusha discussed, a man from Vaseelyevac, riding on a little horse with a wooden saddle, was approaching them. When he came to the women, he stopped the horse and greeted them in the name of God.

"Do you know Mr. Stevan's house?" he asked.

"I know. I'm his wife," replied Staniya, confused.

"I'm from Vaseelyevac, and I had to attend a little work in Dobry Do. There in the municipality, they gave this letter to bring it to you." The man stretched out his hand in the coat pocket and pulled out the letter from there.

"And who is it from?" asked Staniya in a trembling voice.

"I do not know, young woman. I cannot read. Find someone to read it for you," replied the man.

"Okay, big thanks to you, good man. Come to my house to have lunch if you're hungry," said Staniya.

"I am not hungry, and I am in a hurry. Thank you. Now stand well with God. I have to get home before it gets too dark." The man and his horse sank into the woods along the narrow country road.

Staniya went to Uncle Krsto's house, and outside the house she called out, "Miruna! Hey, Miruna!"

Miruna came out. "Come on, Staniya. Come inside."

"Is your Masho at home?" asked Staniya.

"He is. Come on. Drop in."

Masho was doing something around the house, and once he saw her, he released the tools and asked, "How have you been, Staniya? What brings you to us?"

"I am okay, but there is always shortage of time. There is always something that pops up, and there is no one else to take care of these things but me. But I come to you to ask you to read this letter for me, if you have time."

"Yes, Staniya, there are always three hundred jobs to attend to. From who is this letter?"

"I do not know, Masho. Poor me, you know I cannot read at all. Please take it and look yourself to see who wrote it to us."

Masho took the letter, looked at it, held it with one hand, and carefully opened it with the other hand.

Staniya had no patience to wait and asked, "Who is it from, Masho?"

"It's from your Stevan, dear. No one else would write to you."

Staniya blushed in her cheeks, and her eyes received a special glow. She refrained from asking anything, and she was eagerly waiting to hear what Masho would say to her.

Masho silently read the letter and then said to Staniya, "It says that Stevan is healthy and well and tells you not to worry about him. He says he was a little weak but is okay now, so he will come home in a few days. He sends his best wishes to you, Vishnya (Višnja), and Rayko (Rajko), and he cannot wait to see you. That's what it says. Now wait every day for when you will see him," said Masho with a kind smile on his face as he passed the letter to Staniya.

A few days of Staniya's anticipation passed. One day a man appeared on a snow-saturated walking path right toward Staniya's home. He wore a military uniform with a long, old overcoat, belt, and no weapons. His left hand was resting on a white, dirty scarf that had been tied around his neck.

Staniya first saw him and quickly ran out of the house. It was not hard for her to recognize her dear Stevan, although so many years had passed since she last saw him.

She quickly returned to the house door and cried joyfully, "Children, your daddy is here!"

The children ran out, and once they saw a military uniform, they paused, staring intently at the soldiers.

"You do not know your dad?" asked Stevan, who had already been standing at the entrance of the house with a smile.

The children were now relaxed and full of love, hugging his neck. After this emotional expression of love, they all went into the house, where they continued their joy and happiness.

Stevan removed white bread from a military bag and cut slices for the children. The children, happily peering, stood in delight and ate. Small Rayko broke off a piece of hard corn bread and began to mix it with white bread. Others started laughing at him, while he felt embarrassed and ran and hid somewhere behind the house.

Stevan was slightly wounded in the left arm above the elbow and had to stay in a hospital in Nish for a few days until his wound was sanitized and he felt better. A few days after arriving home, he took off the cloth on which his arm rested and began tackling work around the house that had already been waiting for him.

Arrest of the Deserters

The deserters Borisav and Mirash had not returned home, although all surviving warriors long ago came to their homes and their loved ones, who had been waiting for them for years. The two deserters had made a dugout near a stream overgrown with tall beech trees. Kravarske Mountain seemed to be the safest and most suitable place to hide. The forest was rich in wild animals, especially roe deer and wild boars. The old, abandoned salt mine, which the ancient Romans might have used, provided them with the necessary supplies and precious ingredients. They were hiding from everything and everyone, especially shepherds who knew them well.

The dugout was well camouflaged. Obscuring it was a huge blackberry bush. A very narrow passage between the bush and pits could not be easily observed. All kinds of things packed the dugout. There were crates and boxes with precious objects, along with weapons, military and civil clothes, rugs, sheets, coffee mills, clocks, various women's jewelry, and tableware. And who knew what else would all be there. All of these things were worthy and skillfully found by deserters at the places where the refugees hid them before leaving their homes, fleeing before the Bulgarian and Arnaut arsonists and robbers, in the uncertainty and hope that they would, if they ever came back alive, again find and use them.

At the creek at Kravarske Mountains, where the dugout was located, the deserters were completely safe at all times from hostile occupiers of the country, especially when the inhabitants of this region were located in Toplica. Completely empty, this area served as a refuge for wild animals, while the Bulgarian troops did not need to patrol there, knowing the people moved somewhere in an unknown direction. Thus Borisav and Mirash were the only masters of the whole of this region until the return of refugees and soldiers from the war. However resettlement of the refugees was something where these bandits took away every last sense of security and peace.

Upon the return of soldiers from the war, the mountains come to life. New homes emerged, nicer and more comfortable than the huts that the elderly and women had raised in a hurry as temporary shelters. There was needed material, which this mountain had plenty. The sound of axes was heard from all sides. People were making slates for roofs and ceilings, along with beams and boards for floors. And they prepared a variety of other building components.

This situation to Borisav and Mirash was not favorable; however, they did not dare to leave their dugout. They spent most of their time hiding there. Between them in those days were frequent home disputes about who was to blame for their current woes and troubles. These arguments would typically begin like this.

"It's all your fault!" Borisav claimed. "If you did not insist we stay here, we would be in the safer place, and I would not be in fear being here every day."

"It's not true!" angrily responded Mirash. "If you had listened to me, we would never have made it here to this damn dugout, but we'd be somewhere on the Radan Mountain, Kukavica, or somewhere safer where no one is banging above your head."

"Do not do anything to defend yourself!" said Borisav. "Because if you were not here, I would have gone with the others through Albania and to Thessaloniki and would not be now hiding from each child in the mountain."

"You are a lying dog!" angrily yelled Mirash. "I told you to go, and you were stuck. You said, 'I am not happy to die through Albania when I can stay here and enjoy the life of wealth that others left. Why should I be crazy to fight?' Is that what your words were? Come on. Tell me!"

Scared by Mirash's anger, Borisav would change his tone. "It makes no sense to argue now. It is what it is. Let's try to find a way out and save ourselves from this situation; otherwise we are stuck here forever. You see that the mountain is full of people, and if anyone sees us, he will stick a loop on our necks."

"For sure we should have thought about it earlier rather than now when we cannot bring our nose out of this hole."

Such squabbles were more frequent with the deserters. They spent more and more time in the dugout, and even in the night, they did not dare to go out.

One day shepherds lost cattle down the mountain toward the creek, near the old salt mine. Shepherds rushed after the cattle and finally came to the clear, mountain stream. Dyoko jumped over the creek and found a large blackberry bush at the end of it. Small, barely perceptible paths ended at the bush, and this made him curious to look wherever it was leading.

When he saw the small door of the roughly cut and dry beech branches, frightened, he chased cattle as fast as possible to get away from this shady place. He could not imagine what was hiding behind the door, but he knew that someone certainly lived there who did not want to be seen and discovered.

Arriving at the village, Dyoko looked for his grandfather Krsto, and once he found him, he ran up to him and said, "Grandpa, I saw the door!"

"What kind of door, you fool? What are you ranting about? Break it down a little bit!" a nervous Uncle Krsto said.

"Doors, Grandfather. A real door. Wooden," continued Dyoko.

"Stop whining and tell me what you saw!" an angry Uncle Krsto said.

"Look, Grandfather. It was like this. Our cattle fled down the mountain, toward the old salt mine. I ran and ran, but I could not catch them. So I chased after them all the way to the creek, where I found them drinking water. I was chasing them up the creek to maneuver them back. And then after a blackberry bush, I saw a door."

"What does a door do in the creek? Who could even take them over there and leave?" wondered Uncle Krsto.

"No one brought them there, Grandfather, but someone made them there ."

While the grandfather and grandson argued, Masho came from somewhere. Seeing the serious faces, he asked, "What are you two arguing so much about?"

"Well, the boy saw some door somewhere in the creek near the salt mines, and he cannot explain it well," the old man said and laughed.

"Where did you see the door, my son?" asked Masho.

"Dad, when I was returning the cattle, I first saw a small walking path. I searched everywhere the path was leading, and I saw a door. Behind the door there must be a room in which someone lives. Well, so I thought, and I quickly chased the cattle and fled."

Masho did not take long to understand the essence of things. As a warrior he immediately assumed that someone was hiding in the dugout, someone who did not want any company.

A few days after that event, a small group of gendarmes escorted Borisav and Mirash to Cat's Rock. Their hands were chained, and they were moving with four horses, well loaded with all kinds of things. In addition to the gendarmes, the group consisted of a number of civilians and well-known villagers, probably those whose goods were contained in loads on horses, that is, stolen by the two bandits during their refuge.

Deserters were moving humbly with bowed heads, not looking at anyone. They were miserable with swollen cheeks, usual for people who spent long times in a dugout and were not exposed to the sun and wind for some time. They did not speak to anyone and were answering questions briefly and quietly.

When a gendarmerie sergeant asked from where they get so much stuff, Borisav, without lifting his head, muttered, "We found them."

"Where did you go to find them, and who lost so much of it?" jokingly asked the sergeant.

"In the woods we found them, and we were afraid that someone might take them," said Mirash.

"It's indeed fair and commendable. Well, you took care and saved the acquired assets of these poor people so no one else could steal them. But why did you not return them to the people when they came back from Toplica? You kept them in the pit to this day. Who knows what else you would have kept if we did not pull you out to the sun from that rat's hole?" asked the sergeant in an ironic tone.

On this question there was no answer. The two deserters were silent and looked anxiously. One of the gatherers asked the sergeant if they would give back the stolen items.

"Everything will be given back, but they first must be submitted to the court as evidence against these degenerates," said the sergeant.

Please Get Married, My Son

August's sun was richly heating Cat's Rock's plateau, as if it wanted to bring more warmth to the hearts of the highlanders. It was melting the ice, which was deposited at the mountain peaks for years. In the air of immense heat, trembling, panting sheep huddled next to each other under an old oak tree and cornfield, dried almost like a desert looking forward to the soothing rain. Nevertheless Cat's Rock looked somewhat reborn and new and smelled of freshness and warmth.

Warriors, who passed many corners of the Balkans during the war and saw the ways of life of other people, wanted their homes to be more beautiful and comfortable. So in the region began to emerge beautiful, snow-white houses, whose prettiness was enhanced by green farms and orchards around them.

It was the time of the harvests, and in front of some homes was a lot of noise of people. Two horses, tied by a long rope to a strong pivot, padded around, trampling mature wheat arranged on the ground. Men and women were raising and shaking the wheat with wooden tools and were then removing empty thatch to be later used for winter feeding of livestock or stuffing of mattresses and pillows. Country land that was not used during the war gave birth that year as never before, and branches with fruit were bent all the way to the ground from the weight.

Lieutenant Radoye came home for holiday and rolled up his sleeves. He was working in the field.

Staniya came from somewhere, and seeing how he did not spare any effort to work around the field, she called out to Radoye, "Have a great work, sir!"

"Thank you, Staniya," Radoye answered without pausing.

"You are a gentleman, but you can also do peasants' tasks?" joked Staniya.

"I can, thanks to God, Staniya, when it's a necessity. What would these two old people do if I did not help a little? A lot of work is waiting to be done."

"That's right, Radoye. I am just joking a little bit with you."

"No worries, Staniya. God gives us the jokes."

Staniya went further with a sickle in hand to cut a bit of leaf for cattle. The last winter cattle ate everything she had, and she wanted to stock up. The more, the better, just in case.

The doors opened, and there appeared Tominka, sweaty with raised ends of scarves over her head. She paused, and once she saw Radoye, she said, "Radoye, my son, you're hungry, my love! Come on. Get something for breakfast. Here I made you cicvara. I know you love to eat this and probably have not eaten this for a long time."

Radoye dropped the tools he was using, got a bucket of water, washed his hands, and then entered the house. On the table were a fresh and warm corn bread, a sooty frying pan with cicvara made of corn flower, young cheese, and kaymak.

While Radoye was having breakfast, Tominka was doing something in the house. During that time, it raced through her head to say to Radoye what she was struggling with. Finally she stopped, folded her arms on her chest, and began, "Radoye, my son, you see that your mother is old and infirm and has hard housework all the time. Marry, my son. Let it rejuvenate our house, and let the cries and laughs of a child be heard here, like in the houses of others in our village. I know it's hard to get over your Pava. It's hard for me too. And I do not think any other daughter-in-law could replace her. But what can you do? The dead do not return, and the alive have to live. Many girls would be happy to marry you, and there are, thanks to God, enough of them in our area so we can choose a good girl that you like."

As she spoke, she sweated all over. This good old woman knew that her Radoye loved Pava so much and it was hard to get over and replace her with any other. It was very difficult for her to mention this to him, but still she had to mention it because they had so much land to be cultivated and inherited by future generations.

Radoye put down the spoon. "I know it's very difficult for you, Mom. I know Uncle Stanko spends most of his time in the field and you are always alone in your housework. I also know that our house needs to rejuvenate. That's why I'm thinking to get married. But to be honest, I do not have a girlfriend so far. We must make sure that I find someone you'd be happy with and for me as God wishes. I'll marry, Mom, so do not worry at all about that."

Radoye much loved his mother, and for him her words fell hard on his soul. Without her there, who knew if he would ever decide to get married? But because of her, he had to do something.

Tominka was both sad and happy with Radoye's words, and she was all in tears. She knew her son would sacrifice because of her, yet she knew how much her request caused pain because he lost the woman he loved so much. She was apparently satisfied with Radoye's response, although she knew that her quest had not broken all spirits and her Radoye would have difficulty in deciding on marriage. She took a deep breath and then turned around and found a curved wooden yoke. She placed a wooden vessel at each end of it and headed to the clear water well located away from her house.

Going slowly toward the well, Tominka was thinking about the conversation with her son. She remembered late Pava, her kindness, and rare beauty that was difficult to see in girls around their region.

Here Is Our Avenger!

On the day of the Feast of the Assumption, people gathered at Uncle Krsto's home to talk and agree on some important rural matters. Radoye had not yet traveled to Nish, so he came to propose to renew sport shooting activity in the village. He promised to personally take care to provide guns, ammunition, targets, and other things this sport needed and the villagers could take care of further organization. The shooting range was not a problem because nature was taking care of that.

While they discussed, proposed, and approved, some of those present cried, "Folks, someone is coming!"

All heads turned to the side the man was coming, and they saw a horseman approaching them via Kravarsko cemetery.

"This person is not from around here," said one of the present villagers.

"I would say so. Where is he heading?" Vasiliye never took his eyes off the horsemen.

"We'll find out soon," Masho noted.

The horseman was approaching nearer to the assembled group of people. He was tall and strong. Dense, black, crisp hair, barely noticeable under a tilted hat, and a small black mustache made this handsome guy manifest gigantic manhood and strength. He wore a new suit from the Shumadiya (Šumadija) region in the Central Serbia, and on his feet he had boots made of fine leather. His beautiful horse was already exhausted from a long distance travelled. All eyes were focused on the horseman, examining carefully who he might be.

Once the newcomer was about fifty meters from the crowd, Uncle Krsto stood up, opened his arms, and went to meet the man, crying joyfully, "Oh, my son Sreten! I have not seen you for such a long time!"

Sreten stood down from the horse, put the reins over his arm, and said, "Uncle Krsto! You are alive, tough, old guy!" Sreten grabbed and kissed him, holding him long into the warm embrace, after which they walked to the group of people.

"Praise God, good people!" greeted all to Sreten.

"May God give you all the best!" Sreten said.

"This is Sreten, people, our brave hero and vigilante, who the Bulgarian thugs and murderers will long remember." Uncle Krsto's eyes became dimmed.

"You overpraise me, old man," said Sreten with a smile. He felt a bit shy with such praise from Uncle Krsto.

"That is Sreten … Sreten," heard were the undertone of words of the gathered people. It was a great name that everyone in this region knew about.

"Hello, Sreten brother!" Radoye approached him. "I heard a lot of good things about you. I am honored here to see you in person and thank you for everything you've done for me and the entire region. I am Radoye, who is much indebted to your bravery." He spread his hands and exchanged fraternal kisses with Sreten.

"Welcome, our lionhearted hero!" Petar approached with open arms, and he exchanged brotherly kisses with Sreten. "All your heroic deeds are known to all of us. My Stoya and others told me so much about you. I thank you from the bottom of my heart."

And the others came and exchanged hugs and brotherly kisses with Sreten.

Then Sreten said, "Brothers, you do not have to thank me so much. I've done what all of you would have done as honest patriots. The Bulgarians were brutal with our children. They were killing, robbing, persecuting, and raping, and they did everything inhuman that came to their minds. I was forced by circumstances found here, and I was unable to silently observe that violence. For violence I was avenging without mercy whenever there was an opportunity to strike at the enemies. I believe it is the duty of every honest man, and to all of you I say, if you were in my position, you would do the same."

Uncle Krsto proposed that Sreten sit down on a new rag that was sprawled on the grass under the old pear tree.

"Take this rag, old man, so it does not stain. I'm better at sitting on this green grass," Sreten said. He pulled out a pack of fine cigarettes from his pocket and offered it to the present people.

As they sat and talked, above them were rising puffs of bluish smoke, which then got lost somewhere in the direction of Bechov Karst.

Masho rolled up his sleeves, and he was skinning a sizeable lamb hung on a plum tree behind the house. Around him gathered children who watched what he was doing, and every now and then, they were bugging him with questions. Women and young people from the village all arrived. All were curiously watching Sreten and admiring his manhood, strength, and appearance. All carefully listened to him, and everyone wanted to personally see and know him.

"So where do you live now in peace, Sreten? Have you rested from the war?" asked Uncle Krsto.

"Well, old man, I am where you can see me. I am almost always on the go, as I was during the war, but without the guns and bombs. I'm officially stationed in Prokuplye (Prokuplje). I'm in charge of a commission for the assessment of war damages, so I came to you to see you and talk. I know you had multiple losses that had perished in this bloody war and you are devastated and burnt worse than anyone in the Toplica region. We have to establish a subcommittee among you that will go from house to a house in your area to list all damages caused by the war. Only we need take into account that this list is not exaggerated, but the data is accurate as far as possible. We should immediately determine literate people amongst you, and I will give you instructions on how to do the job."

"Here, I would suggest Masho," Radoye said. "He is quite literate and just. He will, I believe, ensure that the job is properly done. Others, suggest who you want."

"I suggest Petar," interrupted Vasiliye. "He is literate and just, and he will do the job fairly."

"I would say that the commission includes Vasiliye. He was the head of the village, and he understands relevant matters very well," Uncle Krsto proposed.

"Do you all agree with these proposals?" asked Sreten.

"Agree! Agree!" cried those present.

"Then when you agree, I agree," said Sreten. "And now the three of you come with me to give you the material and brief you on what and how you need to write."

Sreten called the selected subcommittee to his horse, and he removed some paper from a leather saddle bag and distributed it. Then he briefly explained how to do the job. And he sent them off to accomplish their task.

Uncle Krsto, who was somehow always located near Sreten, asked, "In God's name, Sreten, are you married? I know you were not married during the war, so I am somehow interested to know if you are still single."

"Yes, Uncle. Now is the same. I am still not married, and who knows when I will get married? Now I do not have time to think about it until the conclusion of important state affairs, and then you will find someone for me because you have more time than me to look around."

"I will, my son. You have just come here at the festival of St. Peter's Day held in Degrmen at Becho's Church to see the kind of girls we have here. They are more beautiful than mountain fairies."

Miruna came out of the house, approached Uncle Krsto, and whispered something in his ear. Then she went back to the house.

Uncle Krsto stood up and said, "Let's go, people, through the door to have a little bit to eat. Here, for God's sake, we are dying of hunger in front of a full house."

"Come on, Sreten. You had a lot of time to get hungry. Our homes are close, and we can eat there if this is not enough." Radoye stood up.

Others began to stand up and started to disperse to their homes.

"Where are you all going for God's sake?" yelled Uncle Krsto.

"Uncle, we are going to our homes. Our houses are so close, so we should not bother you with the lunch," said Radoye.

"This is not nice that you leave this great man alone. Please stay and honor our favorite guests! It would be a shame to leave, so please stay and make him a little company."

This scolding from the old man was like lightning, and they all quickly came into the house and sat for the lunch. They saw steamed lamb roast on a large beech table, and its pleasant scent tickled everyone's nose. A few bottles of rakiya were placed on the table. Sreten and Radoye sat at the head of the long table, and the others sat down in a determined order, which these highlanders strictly took into account.

"When did you manage to prepare so much food, in God's name?" Stevan pointed to the hot pan with lamb roast.

"Well, my Miruna is so capable that she prepared all this by herself," cheerfully replied Uncle Krsto.

There was a little lull, and Uncle Krsto used that situation to ask the guests to fill up their glasses. He then lifted the glass, saying, "Thank you, brothers. We came here to talk and joke about things as neighbors and friends, and we meet here to see our dear guest, who did a lot for us at our end. Thank you all and you, my dear Sreten, who did not spare any effort to come and see the poor people in our hills, your acquaintances, and those you did not meet before. Today's meeting with you made me feel rejuvenated and gave me hope in life.

"This moment reminds me of all of our earlier meetings on those tough days in which you were watching over us and avenged for all the evils the enemy had done. I wish you the best health and happiness, my dear Sreten! May God give you the best luck, no matter of your location."

The old man drank a glass of drink to the bottom, and then others followed his example. They ate and drank, and the atmosphere became livelier and noisier as they recounted the experiences of war, suffering and distress in camps, fraternal acceptance, wedding parties and funerals in Gojinovac, and other memories and events.

Sreten clearly avoided talking about his experiences because he believed, all of that he know, there was no need to talk about. He listened with great pleasure to Radoye when he spoke of how he and Petar silenced heavy Bulgarian machine gun at the Salonika Front.

In the early evening, the subcommittee returned from the field and made the final records with Uncle Krsto and other people who were present there. Once they finished they passed the document to Sreten, who, after careful examination, packed and placed it in his bag. Then he stood up, said good-bye to everyone, and went toward Prokuplye.

Comment of the Authors

I created *The Refugees* as part of my desire to connect generations of young people and their ancestors and inform future generations about the tragedies that war can cause, all through a story of events in the Toplica area during the Great War (First World War). All this is through

Grandpa Milich Dragovich

a story about ordinary people and their lives and sufferings during that period. A special wish I have is that, through this novel, a message is sent to people to proudly remember their history and carefully protect their roots, patriotism, and philanthropy, as our ancestors did.

The novel tells us about ordinary people, peasants actually, caught by torment and suffering that the Great War brought in Serbia and Toplica. The Serbs had not rested well since the Balkan Wars, and their destiny already brought new troubles and evils. Most of the men of the military age were recruited, while children, elderly, and women remained at their houses. So to speak, there was no one to protect them from the brutality of the aggressor's forces, militias, and bandits. The only way to protect them was to go to the refugee camps once it was no longer possible to remain in their homes.

The novel describes the sufferings of these people, but also the heroic blood of the Serbs that opposed to, as they could, a far more superior enemy. The novel describes common people and their grief for loved fathers and sons, husbands, brothers, and men who were far away at the Salonika Front. The novel describes new friendships, love, human qualities, philanthropy and brotherhood, and courage, but also includes the baseness that people are prone to.

At the same time, the novel is aligned with the historical facts of that period and mentions significant figures of that time, such as Kosta Voyinovich (Kista Vojinović) and Kosta Milovanovich Pechanac (Kosta Milovanović Pećanac).

I have written the novel based on the memories and records of my grandfather, Milich Dragovich (Milić Dragović). During his life Grandpa Milich told me so much about his childhood, including life in the Upper Kosanica, Becho's Church (Bećova crkva), Ivan Tower (Ivan kula), Devil's Town (Đavolja varoš), everyday life of adults and children, nature, an old oak three, wild animals, and a dog that carefully watched the herd and farm of the Dragovich family in Prekorodye. It's an unforgettable experience with this wonderful man. His memories delighted me, along with papers on which he wrote various details. For several years I have carefully studied, comparing it with the historical facts, and dealt with this in this novel.

Grandpa Milich was born in 1909 in Prekorodye in Upper Kosanica from the father of Dragovich and mother of Carichich (Caričić) family from Merdare. He spent his earliest days in his area, so as a child, he went through as a Toplica refugee during the Great War. After the war he entered the military school system as a young boy, and upon graduation he served as a gendarmerie sergeant in Eastern Bosnia and Western Serbia.

In the meantime the family Dragovich, due to the difficult living conditions in the mountainous areas after the war and the state's call for the Serbs to return to their holy Kosovo with a variety of assistance and benefits, settled in the village of Slivovo near the city of Uroshevac (Uroševac). World War II found Grandpa Milich in Vishegrad (Višegrad), where, agitated by the Ustasha crimes against the people of Bosnia, he joined Serbian military forces. During the war he moved to Kosyerich (Kosjerić) in Western Serbia and then went to the front in Veliko Gradishte (Veliko Gradište) and Eastern Serbia.

When the war ended, although he was eager to return to his Toplica, the heartland of the Dragovich family, there was no longer anyone. So he went to Kosovo and settled in Uroshevac near his most loved, where he worked as a lawyer and chief of the municipal economy until his retirement.

Great-grandson Stefan at his grandfather's and grandmother's grave

During old age he experienced the same tragedy as the beginning of his life. In 1999, a few months after the signing of the Kumanovo Agreement, Grandfather and his wife Milesa went to a new refuge, first in the former Yugoslav republic of Macedonia, the only possible way to escape from Uroshevac and repression of Albanian militia. And with the help of the Red Cross, we managed to find them and move them to Serbia proper, to the city of Kosjerić.

Soon Grandfather died, and Grandmother followed a few weeks later. He never passed the desire for his Prekorodye and Toplica, although he loved Kosovo with all his heart. He was buried in Prolom Spa (Prolom Banja), next to his wife Milesa, at the local cemetery in his beloved Topolica.

I want to thank all the nice people who helped turn this work to reality. I must emphasize gratitude to Toplica National Museum in Prokuplje on the historical photo material presented in this novel. Unmetered thanks go to Mr. Darko Zarich (Darko Zarić), historian and senior curator of the museum in Prokuplje, for comments and validation of historical facts mentioned in the novel. Also big thanks to Mr. Marko Lopushina Marko Lopušina), news correspondent and writer, for professional tips; Professor Akexandar Andreyevich (Aleksandar Andrejević), rector of the Educons University, for his support; as well as the team from the publishing house.

I hope and wish the readers a pleasant experience of reading this novel.

Dr. Daniel Churchill (AKA Zvezdan Ćurčić)
Professor, The University of Hong Kong, Hong Kong

Comments of the Historian

The Refugees is the story of ordinary people in an uprising in Toplica in 1917 against the then-world military powers of Austria-Hungary, Germany, and Bulgaria and the fate of people after the failure of the unrest in fleeing their village of Cat's Rock to the village of Gojinovac.

The Toplica uprising was the only one in Europe in any territory occupied by the army of the Central Powers. Popular discontent and indignation caused by the Bulgarian army's recruitment of the military-age Serbian population in early February 1917 resulted in mass flight to the mountains in front of the Bulgarian recruitment committee. These were as rebels, led by Lieutenant Kosta Voyinovich and Reserve Infantry Lieutenant Kosta Milovanovich Pechanac.

Rebels created the so-called Chetnick state based in Prokuplye, which stretched north to south in an area of about eighty square kilometers of territory and the front line of defense of two hundred and forty kilometers. The territory was defended by 12,762 rebels on foot and 364 horsemen who were armed with old rifles, 150 bullets, and a bomb. About sixty thousand soldiers of the Central Powers attacked the Chetnick state and had broken the resistance of the rebels soon after. And after twenty days of the state, it ceased to exist on March 25, 1917. Before the onslaught of the enemy, the insurgent army itself split apart into small groups of rebels who were hiding in the woods of the Toplica and Yablanica regions.

During the suppression of the uprising, the occupier had done serious crimes. Crimes of the Bulgarian occupiers were much higher once they went in pursuit of the rebels. People were fleeing from the Bulgarian army, who were slaughtering, cutting off body parts, burying people alive, and raping. Slavs (Bulgarians and Serbs) had—at yet another time in history—been killing each other at the instigation of the Germans (Austrians and Germans). Going to the refugee camp meant the only salvation in many cases. The villagers of Cat's Rock chose the refuge as the only option to survive.

The ruthless occupier had burned fifty-five villages and fifty-five thousand objects. After the war, International Survey Commission counted twenty thousand Serbs killed in the uprising and the aftermath. The occupiers committed genocide, the only word that could apply to these crimes. Most were civilians killed in the uprising.

Uncle Krsto below Bechov Karst, as he learned that the neighboring village of Trpeze was burned, led the residents of Cat's Rock in the refuge. Refugees at Devil's Creek experienced one of the horrors of the war, rape of women by the occupiers. Participating refugees happily came to their friends in the village of Gojinovac, where they waited for the end of the war.

Revenge is an integral part of the war, and it made a Chetnick, Sreten, kill the Bulgarian rapists. Sreten avenged Pava, who Bulgarian soldiers killed, and others who suffered during the rape at Devil's Creek.

In the refuge love was born between Stoya, a girl who the Bulgarian soldiers raped, and Radosh from Gojinovca. Shortly after the wedding of two young people, refugees returned to the burnt ruins of their homes and restored them back again, continuing life in their village. People were returning life to some village, but not to the graves. After the war ended, the Serbian army men from the front—Pava's husband Radoye, Uncle Krsto's only son Masho, Staniya's husband Stevan, and so forth—returned to the village. Life itself had returned to Cat's Rock.

"There is no freedom without blood. We have to fight to the last," said Kosta Voyinovich.

Serbs from Toplica and Yablanica fought to the last. These areas gave the best first and second recruits of the Iron Regiment in spreading the glory of the Serbian army in the Great War. In the Toplica uprising in 1917, the participants were Serbs who did not want war, those who were left wounded in their homes after the famous battle of Cer and Kolubara, those who were too young or old for the military, and women. In short, the Serbs of Toplica and Yablanica were all participants in the Great War, regardless of gender and age.

When opening the monument commemorating killed Toplica people in the Great War on September 9, 1934, His Holiness Patriarch Mr. Varnava said,

Toplica, the name of the great and glorious, the unreserved merit and work of its sons, in all eras of our history, performed at the pinnacle of glory and greatness, the fateful period of World War I it became a major symbol of Serbian heroism, unequaled trophy of Serbian glory, unattainable example of sublime martyrdom of a nation. History of Toplica is great miniature of history of our entire nation.

War, refuge, grave sufferings, emigration, and immigration are monuments of the history of Toplica and the Serbian people. It's the history of the inhabitants of a village in Kosanica, Cat's Rock. It's memories of Milich Dragovich, reminiscent of the novel to that history. Grandpa Milich told this story to his grandson Daniel Churchill (Zvezdan Ćurčić), and he published it in this novel. Dr. Churchill did what we should all do, listen to the stories of his grandfather and great-grandfather and then write and publish. Writing it means not to forget it. It's a sin not to record memories of these heroic men in the Great War.

The value of this narrative sources is that there is some new information about life in the uprising, the new rebels (Sreten), the new soldiers and noncommissioned officers of the Iron Regiment (Stevan, Masho, and Radoye), and new victims (Pava and the raped women of Cat's Rock). In short, it's everything that is not in the sources of the first order.

Memories of Milich Dragovich gave us new information about the uprising. On the participation of residents from Cat's Rock in the uprising so far, we had no data. These are the first data, so these memories of Milich Dragovich are of great value for the history of the Toplica uprising.

Darko Zharich (Darko Žarić)
Historian, Senior Curator
Toplica National Museum in Prokuplye, Serbia

About the Author

Daniel Churchill (a.k.a. Zvezdan Ćurčić) is a professor at the University of Hong Kong. He specializes in education, immigration,

refugee law, and practice. He is also a migration law agent registered with the Australian government. Through his life and career, he developed a strong interest and passion for issues affecting civilians at war, refugees and their needs, and improvements in human conditions through education.

Born in Kosovo, the southern province of Serbia, he witnessed conflicts in his lifetime with tragic outcomes on civilians. Stories of his grandfather, who was a refugee at the beginning and then again at the end of the twentieth century, strongly shaped his understanding of the issues and events he describes in his writing. Furthermore his work through the immigration law activities with refugees from all over the affected world allows Professor Churchill to develop global understanding of conditions and human suffering raging at various parts of the globe, even today.

16299066R00085

Printed in Great Britain
by Amazon